ABOUT THE AUTHOR

In 2000, Holly Jacobs sold her first book to Harlequin Enterprises. She's since sold more than twenty novels to the publisher. Her romances have won numerous awards and made the Waldenbooks bestseller list. In 2005, Holly won a prestigious Career Achievement Award from *Romantic Times BOOKreviews*. In her nonwriting life Holly is married to a police lieutenant, and together they have four children. Visit Holly at www.HollyJacobs.com, or you can snail-mail her at P.O. Box 11102, Erie, PA 16514-1102.

Books by Holly Jacobs

HARLEQUIN AMERICAN ROMANCE
1232—ONCE UPON A THANKSGIVING
1238—ONCE UPON A CHRISTMAS

HARLEQUIN EVERLASTING
17—THE HOUSE ON BRIAR HILL ROAD

SILHOUETTE ROMANCE
1557—DO YOU HEAR WHAT I HEAR?
1653—A DAY LATE AND A BRIDE SHORT
1683—DAD TODAY, GROOM TOMORROW
1733—BE MY BABY
1768—ONCE UPON A PRINCESS
1777—ONCE UPON A PRINCE
1785—ONCE UPON A KING
1825—HERE WITH ME

This one's for the real officers
of the Erie Police Department, who put so much on
the line every day to keep my favorite city safe. And
to a certain captain who, I'll confess, is my favorite!

"Now, Carly, why would you think I don't dance?" Chuck asked

"I don't know. It doesn't seem very macho. I mean, when I think cops, I think guns drawn, kicking in the door and taking down the...perps?"

He laughed. "Call me a Renaissance man, because I can draw a weapon *and* lead a pretty woman around on the dance floor." He twirled her once, twice. "So, is this our song?" Chuck asked, joking.

Carly must not have noticed the humor in his question, because he could feel her body get tense.

"Chuck, we won't be together long enough to have a song, remember?"

He should probably kick himself for asking something like that. It broke all his keep-things-light rules. Instead of backtracking, he said, "Whether we're together or not, we can have a song. Tell you what, every time I hear Jimmy Buffett, I'll think of you."

"Oh, so we won't just have a song, we'll have a whole singer?" Her tone was light, and her body relaxed—she sort of melted into him. "And I guarantee that I will think about you, about this moment, every time I hear Buffett."

They didn't talk any more after that...they didn't need to. Even when the band switched to a faster song, they continued dancing, swaying to a beat it felt as if only they were following.

Dear Reader,

Saying no is hard.

I know it's not just me. A lot of my friends find it difficult to say no, as well. Carly Lewis, our heroine, has always had a problem with saying the word. And somewhere along the line, as she said yes to everything and put everyone's needs ahead of her own, she lost herself.

In *Once Upon a Valentine's*, Carly is desperately trying to discover who she is. Carly thinks that means she has to stand on her own two feet. Alone. But her friends Samantha and Michelle teach her that she can lean on friends without feeling guilty. And maybe Chuck Jefferson can convince her that she can be whoever she wants to be, as long as she lets him stand by her side. Maybe this is the one time when saying no isn't in Carly's best interests?

I've got to confess, I've really loved visiting Erie Elementary with this trilogy. Watching Samantha *(Once Upon a Thanksgiving)*, Michelle *(Once Upon a Christmas)* and Carly *(Once Upon a Valentine's)* form a friendship that can withstand kids, jobs, new loves—and even the PTA Social Planning Committee—was so much fun. I hope you enjoy this last installment and will watch for my next Superromance novel, available later this year. You can drop by my Web site, www.hollyjacobs.com, for updates, or drop me a line at P.O. Box 11102, Erie, PA 16514-1102!

Happy Valentine's!

Holly

Once Upon a Valentine's
HOLLY JACOBS

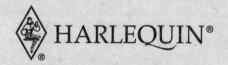

TORONTO • NEW YORK • LONDON
AMSTERDAM • PARIS • SYDNEY • HAMBURG
STOCKHOLM • ATHENS • TOKYO • MILAN • MADRID
PRAGUE • WARSAW • BUDAPEST • AUCKLAND

Recycling programs
for this product may
not exist in your area.

ISBN-13: 978-0-373-75251-5
ISBN-10:   0-373-75251-2

ONCE UPON A VALENTINE'S

Copyright © 2009 by Holly Fuhrmann.

www.eHarlequin.com

Printed in U.S.A.

Prologue

Carly Lewis threw her books into her bag and hollered, "Sean. Rhiana. If you're not in the car in two minutes I'm leaving without you."

She heard hurried scuffles and groaned responses from upstairs and knew her two seventh-graders believed her warning. She actually had followed through on this particular threat last year, right after she and the kids had moved from their upscale Millcreek subdivision to the small bungalow on Erie's upper east side. They'd been running late, and she'd had enough and left without them.

Of course, even though their school was within walking distance, she'd felt guilty seconds after she'd pulled out of the driveway so—soft touch that she was—she'd simply circled the block. She'd pulled back in front of the house and found them standing there. They looked so much alike they could be actual twins rather than siblings born ten months apart. They'd appeared so forlorn and unsure. And as always, simply looking at the two of them melted her heart.

As they'd climbed into the car she'd told them that next

time she wasn't coming back and they'd be forced to walk to school. They seemed to take the threat seriously, which helped with her rather hectic morning schedule. But she knew she'd always come back. That's just what mothers did.

"One minute," she called as she surveyed her bag, hoping she'd remembered everything.

Thirty-two and finishing her nursing degree—it's not what she'd intended. Thankfully, almost all her old credits had carried over. If she could get through this last term, she'd have it made. She'd have her degree in December and in the new year she'd be ready to start a new life.

The life of a single, self-supporting college graduate and mother.

The phone rang.

Carly glanced at her watch. And even though she knew she shouldn't, that a phone call this early was never good news and answering it was probably a mistake, she picked the portable up. She wasn't any more able to walk away from a ringing phone than she was able to drive away and leave her kids. "Hello?"

"Hi, Carly. It's Heidi."

Answering the phone wasn't just a mistake, it was a huge tactical error. One she might never recover from.

Heidi.

She didn't have to ask Heidi who.

Heidi.

The PTA President for the last three years.

Heidi.

The perfect, terminally optimistic, sunny force of nature who practically ran Erie Elementary.

Carly's sense of dread intensified as she realized she'd missed last night's first PTA meeting of the year. And the fact that Heidi was calling this morning said that missing it had been a bad, bad mistake.

"I'm about to leave for school, Heidi. Juggling the kids, work, a nursing internship and classes is about killing me. Can I call you back later?"

Like when hell froze over.

Yep, that would be about the time she'd return Heidi's call.

"It will only take a moment," Heidi said fast, as if she was afraid if she didn't spit the words out quickly, Carly would hang up on her. "I'm sending a packet home with the kids. It will have everything you need to get started."

Carly didn't want to ask because asking would make it real, but to her horror the words slipped out of her mouth.

"Get started with what?"

Chapter One

"It will be a cakewalk. You'll simply go in front of the judge and waive your rights to a preliminary hearing. Then the assistant district attorney will tell him we've come to a plea agreement, and the judge will tap his gavel and it will all be over."

"It's that simple?" Carly asked, her voice echoing in the marble-tiled Erie County Courthouse hallway. She'd never been in the building before, and while she hoped she never had a reason to be in it again, she couldn't help but admire its classic, stately beauty.

"It's that simple." Her attorney, Henry Rizzo, was an Erie Elementary parent, albeit a recent one. His daughter, Izzy, was in the second grade, and cute as a button. "Really, Carly, it will be fine. It's not like you habitually set your neighbor's shed on fire. It was a one-time accident and you've already paid the restitution."

"That's true." Three weeks ago, Carly had thought she was putting her past behind her.

Well, she'd certainly managed that, though not in the manner she'd anticipated.

She glanced nervously around the room, and found two cops sitting in the back. The cute young patrol officer—she thought his name was Masterson—who'd been so nice and understanding when he'd taken her to the police station. And the other one. The one who'd arrived on the scene first and stood with her during one of the lowest moments of her life, as she watched her shed and her neighbor's go up in flames.

Lieutenant Jefferson. She'd never forget his name.

He was taller than her—which was no shock, since everyone in the world seemed taller than her five feet and three inches—but he wasn't too tall. Maybe five eight? His plain brown hair was military-length short, but looked as if it would be soft to the touch. For a moment, at the fire, as he'd walked toward her, she'd stopped crying and simply admired the view. But then the fire truck pulled up and the officer had made it apparent he wasn't overly sympathetic to her plight.

All she could think of now, as she looked at him, was that he'd been there that day and that he'd seen her cry. By the time the young cop had arrived on the scene, she'd gotten herself under control, but Lieutenant Jefferson had witnessed her sobs. And she didn't cry pretty like they did in the movies. She was the type of person whose face and eyes turned red while her nose ran like a spigot. The only other person who'd ever witnessed her cry like that was her ex on what had been *the* absolute lowest day of her life.

Carly didn't normally cry. She actually avoided it at all costs, but sometimes it was the only thing left to do.

"Carly Lewis," a bailiff called from the courtroom door, interrupting her sad memory.

"That's us." Henry rose to his feet and waited for her.

Carly stood as well, and tried to ignore the wobbly feeling

in her legs. Appearing in front of a judge wasn't something she was accustomed to.

She wasn't sure what to expect—maybe a television, Perry Masonish sort of courtroom, something in keeping with the grandeur of the hallway. What she found instead was a smallish room that looked as if any kind of business was conducted in it. There were a few ordinary tables, some chairs, and people milling about.

The man sitting behind a raised bench wasn't precisely what she'd imagined, either.

In Carly's mind a judge should be gray-haired with wire-rimmed glasses and a kindly but tough expression.

The judge was her age. In his mid-thirties tops. He had unruly-looking brown hair that looked as if, given a little more length, it might curl. Henry said Judge Anderson Bradley was tough, but fair. She hoped so.

Carly concentrated on following Henry to one of the two tables in front of the judge's bench.

The ADA, Jacqueline Kelly, smiled at her as she walked by. The woman had an abundance of dark hair that would have overwhelmed Carly's petite frame. But on the very tall Jackie the straight, long hair lent an air of warrior woman. And Carly was glad they'd reached an agreement before coming into the courtroom, because Ms. Kelly looked as if she'd be an intimidating opponent.

Things unfolded just as Henry had said. As Ms. Kelly laid out the plea agreement, Carly felt some of her tension ease. It was going to be all right.

She'd already paid Julian, next door, for the shed she'd accidently burned down. Actually, he'd been downright sweet about the whole thing. He'd gone through a difficult divorce three years ago, and said he totally understood wanting to make a fresh start. That's what his move to Pennsylvania had been, a fresh start.

"No," the judge said in a loud, clear voice. "That is not acceptable."

"Pardon?" the ADA asked politely.

Carly looked at Henry, who looked as confused as she felt.

"Mrs. Lewis, would you please stand?"

Carly obliged, feeling a jolt of nerves. She tried to tell herself the judge was only a man, but sitting there in his robes he was intimidating.

"Ms. Lewis, you burned down your neighbor's shed. Do you realize you could have burned down your entire neighborhood with your stunt?"

She nodded. "Yes, Your Honor, and I'm so very sorry."

"I'm sure you are. Being brought before me tends to make many criminals sorry. However, there's no excuse for your wanton disregard of your neighbor's property, as well as your inability to comprehend that your act might have unforeseen consequences."

Carly was willing to apologize, was willing to take her browbeating as stoically as possible, but the judge glaring down at her in his oh-so-condescending way didn't seem to understand. "Pardon me for saying so, Your Honor, but there is an excuse."

"Do tell," Judge Bradley commanded with definite sarcasm in his voice.

"You see, I was dating Dean when my parents died. In hindsight, I suspect losing my family had something to do with why I married him—I was only twenty and felt so alone. I was a junior in college, and he was a senior. I got pregnant almost immediately, and I quit school to work full-time and put him through law school. I was supposed to go back to college and finish my last year as soon as Dean passed the bar, but he said he needed me at home, supporting him, and that my working so much would short-change the kids—we had two by then—and so I should stay home. I thought I'd go back and finish my degree after they got older—"

Judge Bradley looked bored. "Mrs. Lewis, I'm sure this would be an interesting story if someone were looking to be entertained. Maybe you should consider writing your auto-biography? I hear memoirs are all the rage. What I want to know is what sort of excuse you have for burning down your neighbor's property?"

"I'm getting to that, sir. I became a *perfect* lawyer's wife. I decorated the *perfect* house Dean insisted we buy even though I hated it. At his prodding, I joined all the appropri-ate organizations. I dedicated my life to my family. Last year, for Dean's birthday gift, I even decided to redecorated his office. It was another piece of perfection, Your Honor. A steel-gray wool carpet."

In her mind's eye, she could still see the room. "I spent months shopping for the perfect antique mahogany desk. The painting. The Tiffany lamp. The only thing that I couldn't find was a couch. Functional but antique. It would be the focal point for the whole room. Four months, Your Honor. I spent four months combing thrift shops and estate sales. Finally, I found it on eBay, and drove to central Ohio to pick it up. Then I spent two weeks putting new fabric on it, a pattern that pulled everything in Dean's office together."

"Is this the couch you burned?" the Judge asked, looking a bit more interested now.

She nodded. "Yes, but we're not quite to that part of the story, sir. You see, I'd finally moved the couch into Dean's office—his office was done. I stopped by with a surprise picnic. He was working late on a big case, and I thought we'd celebrate. And that's when it happened." She paused, the horrible sight still fresh in her mind, still able to cause her pain.

"Mrs. Lewis?"

"It was six o'clock," she said softly, lost in that moment. "I walked in with dinner in my hands. His reception area was empty, but that wasn't a surprise. I hadn't expected to find anyone there that late. I opened his inner office door and…sir, I smiled. I looked at the beautiful office I'd worked so hard on for Dean—I saw his desk and the wall of law books behind it. It looked so stately, so perfect, then a movement caught my eye and there they were."

"Who?"

"My husband and his secretary…on the couch." She stopped as the embarrassment, the humiliation, the shock of that moment hit her again. "On *my* couch. On the couch I spent months searching for. The couch I'd driven to Ohio to get. There was Dean, with his secretary. *Together* with his secretary, if you know what I mean. How much of a cliché is that? His secretary."

"I'm not sure I follow. How does catching your husband and his secretary together offer an excuse for arson?"

"Your Honor, when my ex and I split our assets, the biggest sticking point was that couch. I wanted it. I was the one who'd found it, who'd put that whole office in order. Dean could keep the rest, but I deserved that couch. He didn't want me to have it because the office was, in fact, wonderful. Eventually he wanted to conclude the settlement more than he wanted a perfect office, so I got the couch."

"And? I do have other cases to hear today, Mrs. Lewis."

"And he brought it to my house the day after Thanksgiving. I had him move it into the backyard. I needed to put that portion of my life to rest. All the bitterness, all the anger. Those kind of emotions can be draining. So, I went into the garage, got the can of gas, poured it on that fabric I'd so painstakingly chosen and I lit it…and well, you know the rest. I only wanted to burn the couch, sir. Not my shed. And certainly not my neighbor's shed. So you can see, burning anything but the couch was an accident."

"An accident brought about by your recklessness," he insisted.

"Yes, sir. It won't happen again."

"I'm sure it won't. And while I have no intention of sending you to jail, because I do believe this was an aberration, I don't think merely making restitution with a year of probation before your record is expunged is enough. So, I sentence you to the restitution and thirty hours community service. Specifically, there's a school district program in January, a safety awareness program. You'll have your nursing degree at the end of this month, I believe I read? You'll be taking your boards in January?"

She nodded.

"Fine. You can go and tell school students in local schools all about the dangers of playing with fire, and whatever other health-related topics the committee would like you to discuss—"

The police lieutenant coughed loudly, causing the judge to stop, as everyone else turned around to glance at him.

Judge Bradley continued, "—and you'll still have time to study for your boards."

"I wasn't exactly *playing* with fire, Your Hon—"

"And I wasn't exactly done, Mrs. Lewis. As a mother, I'm sure you've taught your children to know better than interrupt while you're speaking. The same rule applies in my courtroom. As I was saying, you can participate in this safety awareness program. Go to the schools, talk to the kids. When the program's over, there will be no probation and your record will be expunged immediately, rather than a year from now. I assume that will make your job interviews go easier?"

She nodded, "I'm sure it will, but sir—"

"Mrs. Lewis, this is open for neither debate nor for argument. Do the community service, and get on with your life. All that's left is for you to say, 'Thank you, Your Honor.'"

Henry, her lawyer, jabbed her in the side. "Thank you, Your Honor," Carly muttered.

"I think you'll find the experience very insightful."

Carly muttered under her breath, "Insightful my a—"

"Pardon me?" the judge barked.

"I said, Thank you, Your Honor." Carly frowned.

"Next case," the judge barked.

Henry hustled her out of the courtroom.

"Carly, I'm sorry," Ms. Kelly said. "Judge Bradley can be…well, unpredictable. Especially this last year or so."

"I'll be fine," Carly assured the woman, who wished her luck and said goodbye, leaving Carly standing with Henry.

"Carly, I'm sorry as well," he said. "Maybe the community service won't be too bad."

"I'm sure it won't," Carly reassured her stricken-looking lawyer.

She pulled herself together and started walking down the hall, ignoring the fact she'd just told Henry a lie.

A big one.

When Heidi assigned her to the PTA Social Planning Committee, it'd turned out to be a stroke of good fortune, but she didn't believe she'd be that lucky again with enforced volunteering.

Safety awareness?

Carly had graduated. She had her nursing degree. She'd done her internship at the hospital. All that was left was passing her boards.

She needed to pass the test first time around.

Carly tried to lay out her January in her mind. She'd have to work at the hospital, study for her boards, plan the PTA Valentine Dance and spend hours talking about fire safety to school children.

Add to that, and most importantly, she had to be there for her kids.

Thinking of her kids reminded her that today was the Christmas Fair. Michelle and Samantha were both working it and expecting her.

She glanced at her watch. She'd better hurry. They were bound to ask how today had gone. She felt better just thinking about the sympathy they'd be bound to give her.

Speaking of sympathy, the lieutenant shot her a glance that seemed to contain more than a bit of that emotion in it.

Carly didn't want his, or anyone else's pity. She purpose didn't make eye contact and hurried past him.

She was going to be just fine.

LIEUTENANT CHUCK JEFFERSON watched as Carly Lewis walked by him. She was a little bit of a thing. Maybe five three, with a good pair of heels. Her dark hair was cut to shoulder-length and swayed from side to side as she stalked down the hall. Still, if her nose stayed that high and it rained, she'd drown. Of course, it was winter in Erie, so rain wasn't likely. Snow was likely, and with the cold shoulder Carly was nudging in his direction, she'd be right at home.

He felt sort of sorry for her, though he knew she wouldn't

like that. He'd been a cop for twelve years and had thought he'd long since grown immune to defendants' sob stories, but something about hers touched him.

No, it wasn't her story, it was her reaction. She wasn't willing to stand by and be a victim. She'd been proactive.

She hadn't meant to burn down her neighborhood.

The day of the fire she'd referred to herself as an accidental arsonist.

He smiled as he thought of the phrase.

Chuck headed through the hall to the door of the judge's private office. Anderson Bradley was still talking to his secretary Joyce and looked up as Chuck walked in. "Didn't know this was one of yours. We didn't need you guys as witnesses, obviously."

"The DA prefers to have us here, even if he suspects he won't need our testimony. And the case wasn't exactly mine. I was only a witness—the first officer on scene—not the arresting officer. I was holding down the fort until the patrol officer could get there."

"I thought desk jockeys like you didn't go out on calls." Anderson laughed as he turned and walked into his inner office.

Chuck followed without invitation. "There was a big pileup on Twelfth Street and everyone else was busy. I was in the neighborhood and stopped to see if I could do anything until the patrol car arrived."

Anderson shrugged off his robe and hung it on a hook next to the door. "Anything else new?" He took his seat.

Chuck sat in the chair opposite Anderson's. "Why'd you do it? Throw out her plea and make her work the program?"

"I'll confess, my sentence wasn't what I'd originally planned. I was going to make it a stiffer penalty. But in the end, I couldn't. And when I saw you, I remembered the program. It's a perfect plan. This way her record is cleared by the end of January."

Chuck didn't bother to try to hide his grin. "She got to you."

"No. I don't let people 'get to me.' I can't. My job—my only concern—is to administer justice, and I think I've done that."

"Your mushy center's showing, Andy," Chuck taunted.

"Don't call me that in here…at all." He glanced at the doorway and his secretary.

"I didn't hear anything," Joyce called.

Chuck called back, "Perjury's a crime."

"I didn't swear any oath," Joyce reminded him. "So it's not perjury."

"You know, most judges get some respect," Anderson groused.

"Hey, we don't want your position going to your head," Chuck said. "But my razzing you is done…for now. I'd better get back to the station."

He stood, went a couple steps, then turned back. "And, Andy, don't worry. I won't spread any rumors about your mushy center. Your gooey middle. Your soft spot for a sob story."

Anderson blustered a response, but Chuck hurried out of the office and shut the door behind him, which made it difficult to discern Andy's words. And he didn't add that he shared Anderson's soft spot for Carly Lewis's sob story.

Remembering her crying at the fire, then her look of stony defiance today, he knew he had a decided soft spot for the tiny woman as well.

He couldn't wait to see her again.

And she didn't know it yet, but she'd be seeing him again soon.

IT HAD BEEN A BUSY week for Carly. The Christmas Fair and her trial had been on Monday, Christmas on Wednesday. She'd had the kids until Christmas Day evening, when Dean had picked them up. He'd have them until Saturday night. That had left Carly plenty of time to work and study.

But it was Friday and she was taking the night off because she deserved it.

She drove along the salt-covered street toward Colao's Restaurant where they'd be having their social committee meeting. Well, not really a meeting. Samantha and Michelle were joining her at the Italian restaurant to celebrate the holiday, and the fact that their committee had successfully completed two-thirds of its duties.

The Thanksgiving Pageant and the Christmas Fair had been huge successes. Samantha and Michelle had each done a great job as coordinator. All that was left was the Valentine's Dance that Carly was in charge of. She only hoped it turned out as well as the first two events. But they'd worry about that at the next official meeting.

Tonight was a night for friends.

Carly had brushed off Samantha and Michelle's questions about her trial at the Christmas Fair. They'd been so busy, and the holiday was almost upon them. She didn't want to worry them. She knew they'd want to hear everything though, and tonight she'd tell them. It would be a relief to vent.

Most of the time she'd simply park her car herself, but tonight, with the snow heaped everywhere, she opted to let the valet park it. She handed him her keys, and took the receipt from him as she hurried in to the restaurant.

Samantha was already there. They'd barely said hello when Michelle bustled in.

"Merry Christmas," Michelle cried as she walked up to

the table balancing boxes. "I have some news. So much news for just a couple days." She took off her glove and waved a finger at them.

"Oh, my—" Samantha stood up and hugged Michelle.

Carly had noticed that Samantha was always hugging someone.

Her kids.

Her friends.

Her boyfriend, Harry.

Carly wasn't as big on the hugging but she was just as thrilled for her friend. "I told you so."

The waitress came up the to table and asked Michelle for her drink order. Carly knew Michelle would order something sensible, like a diet soda. This was definitely not a diet-soda sort of celebration. "Champagne, please. We're celebrating our friend's Christmas engagement."

"Congratulations," the waitress said, and moved.

Michelle slid into the booth. "There's more."

"More than you're engaged?"

"The test results came." Michelle was raising her nephew ever since her sister Tara had died. Tara had never told her son who his father was. Last fall, at thirteen, Brandon thought he'd found his dad, a man named Daniel McLean. Daniel and Tara had been friends many years before and had had a one-night stand. Daniel and Brandon hadn't been willing to wait until the DNA test came in, and Michelle wasn't willing to allow a stranger to be alone with her nephew, which is why the three of them were inseparable. At least that's why in the beginning.

Carly and Samantha knew the question of paternity wasn't all that was keeping them together now.

"And?" Carly was about to explode waiting for Michelle to get to the point.

"Daniel *is* Brandon's father. It sort of seemed anticlimactic, if you know what I mean. After all, we knew that Daniel was Brandon's father no matter what the test showed."

"Oh, I think I'm going to cry." Samantha got a tissue from her purse and started sniffling.

Michelle stared at Samantha's hand. "Oh…Samantha?"

Carly watched as Samantha looked down at her hand. And that's when Carly saw it…a ring.

More specifically, an engagement ring.

"Us, too," Samantha admitted, wiggling her finger.

"Geez, this is turning into a freakin' wedding show," Carly teased.

Well, mainly she was teasing. Mostly, she was thrilled that her friends were happy, but, to be honest, the idea of marriage made her stomach do a little flip. She couldn't imagine ever trusting a man enough to marry again.

Carly's trust in Dean had obviously been misplaced. She tried to tell herself that she couldn't measure all men by what her ex had done, but…

That but was always there. And as long as there was a *but,* she'd be better off on her own.

Still, she wasn't going to let her own cynicism taint her friends' engagements. The waitress arrived with the champagne and glasses.

"When dinner's over, bring the check to me," Carly told her, "since it appears we're celebrating not just one, but two Christmas engagements."

"And will you be back to celebrate a third?" The waitress grinned as she poured the champagne, as if everyone in the world should be married. As if marriage was the pinnacle of any woman's aspirations.

"The day I come in and tell you I'm engaged is the day you'll know hell has officially frozen over." Carly tried to smile, hoping it would appear she was joking. But in her heart, she wasn't joking.

Michelle seemed to buy her act. "Carly, if you'd asked me a month ago I'd have told you it was never going to happen to me, yet here I am, head over heels."

"And me," Samantha added. "If you'd asked me at the start of the school year, I'd have told you I planned to avoid men like the plague. And yet…" Samantha wiggled her ring finger at Carly. "Maybe it's the committee. Two of our social activities done, and two of us are engaged. Carly, I hate to point it out, but you have the most romantic event of them all."

Carly drained her glass and set it down with a thud, then poured another. "Let me repeat, when hell freezes over."

Samantha's smile started to slip.

Carly wanted to kick herself. She should be cheering her friends' happiness on, not raining on their engagement parades. She raised her glass. "To happily-ever-afters for all of us."

And Carly knew a happily-ever-after for her involved remaining single.

Permanently.

She wisely didn't add that part, as they all clinked their glasses.

"So, tell us about your hearing," Samantha said. "We've blathered on about happily-ever-afters and engagements long enough."

"Yes, I'm sorry. You didn't say much at the Christmas Fair. It wasn't so bad?"

"Well, it didn't go quite the way we thought it would, you see…"

Carly had planned to be stoic. She wanted to hear about the holiday her friends were having with the new men in their lives, but Michelle's question opened the floodgates, and the words tumbled over one another as Carly told Samantha and Michelle all about the sentencing. "…and that is why I have to meet with some stupid public relations police officer at the station on Monday."

Back in September, when Heidi had called and told Carly she'd assigned the three moms who'd missed the PTA's first general meeting to the Social Planning Committee—the one committee no one on Erie Elementary PTA ever wanted—Carly had been seriously annoyed.

But over the last three months, Carly's meetings with Samantha and Michelle had been a lifeline. Something she counted on, that she looked forward to.

"Carly, I'm sorry," the oh-so-sensible and placid Michelle said. The tall blonde was a sea of tranquility. The only time Carly had seen that unflappableness flap was when Michelle's nephew, Brandon, had wanted to find his real father. That one time, Michelle had seemed scared and confused. Scared that if Brandon did find his father, he'd be hurt. And she'd hesitantly confessed that she was afraid of losing custody of her nephew to a stranger.

Then she'd had a total melt-down when Brandon turned up with his suspected father in tow. But things had turned out well. Michelle had not only come to grips with the idea of sharing Brandon, she'd fallen for Daniel McLean.

"I know you're sorry," Carly told Michelle. "Thanks. I really needed to vent."

"I'm sorry, too," Samantha said. "Have another roll…piece of bread. I love whatever they season the olive oil with."

"What happened to the diet?" Carly asked as she took a slice of bread and dipped it into the warm oil.

"Harry said he likes a woman with curves, and I've decided I'm happy to oblige. I'm no longer trying to lose weight, but I'm going to try not to gain any. Maintain the status quo. That's my new mantra."

"How about the whole sucking the stomach in thing?" Carly teased. Back in September, Samantha had confessed her new exercise plan consisted of sucking her stomach in all day in place of crunches.

"Now, that I'm sticking with. I have abs of steel…with just a bit of padding over them." She laughed.

Samantha had been doing a lot of laughing ever since Thanksgiving and admitting fighting her attraction to Erie Elementary's new principal, Harry Remington. When Samantha's assistant, the third-grade teacher, Mrs. Tarbot, got ill and it meant the entire Thanksgiving Pageant was in Samantha's hands, Harry had stepped up to help. Now he was becoming an integral part of Samantha's family. Even her four kids were getting used to having Harry around. Happiness practically radiated off her, and Carly was glad for Samantha.

"I'll have to spend my January working with a bunch of cops and firefighters on some safety program. I'm supposed to talk about the dangers of playing with fire."

"You weren't playing when you lit that couch on fire," Michelle said.

"You're right, I wasn't. Dean and I had been divorced for months, despite the fact we hadn't settled the custody or division of assets, but he got an order of bifurcation so he'd be able to get engaged to his secretary while we spent months bifurcating all over the place."

"Bifurcating?" Samantha asked. "That doesn't sound right."

"I'm pretty sure I'm using the word wrong. For us, it meant Dean could have his divorce before we worked out all the terms. You can be officially unmarried, and still sorting the details. I'll confess, I just liked how the word sounded, and Dean did his best to make the process as hard as possible. More than once I wanted to tell him to go bifurcate himself."

Michelle and Samantha both laughed, which made Carly smile, some of her ire easing off.

She'd been angry for so long. Angry that she'd given up so many things for Dean, and he'd so casually thrown her away once she'd served her purpose. Angry he could forget the vows they'd made so long ago. Angry that he could walk away from her and the kids so easily.

"Honey," Samantha said, her voice laced with concern. "You can't be angry with him forever."

"The truth of the matter is, I'm not. I told myself that I was burning that couch as a way of purging my past, letting go of the anger and the hurt. And I think I did. I think I'm over Dean Lewis. The problem is, I don't have a couch to burn to get over being mad at myself. I need a change. More than the haircut I got the other day."

She'd gone into the hair salon and asked them to cut off all her hair, wanting—no needing—to do something more to break from the past. The stylist thought the new style suited her.

"Carly?" Samantha asked softly.

She ran a hand through her spiky hair. "I let it happen. I don't know how, I don't know why. I just let him take over. It wasn't any big decision, you know. Just little ones. *Don't cut your hair so short. I like it longer,* he'd say. So, I let it grow out."

"I really like the new do, it suits you," Samantha said, and Michelle agreed.

"Thanks," she said and paused. "Then he just pecked away. Piece by piece. *Honey, I don't know if I can do law school and work...* So, I quit college to financially support us. I planned to go back and get my nursing degree when he passed his bar exam, but it was the kids, and *honey, I really need you to stand by me while I get my practice off the ground.* Then it was joining the right club, volunteering with the right organizations, befriending the right people, decorating in the right way... And the problem was, the right way was never my way. I love color. Big, bright, bold color. Our house was in tasteful neutrals, and if I was really wild, a pastel or two. That's the problem, I guess. That's the anger. I let myself fade from a vivid color to a washed-out imitation."

"The divorce was final months ago. You've divided the assets, so it's finished. You've graduated, and you'll take your boards and be official," Samantha said. "Your future is just a few weeks away, waiting for you. You can decide your own color, Carly. You can be as vivid as you want."

"But... I can't seem to get back to the color I was before Dean."

"Of course you can't," replied Michelle. "You're different now. The thing is knowing you're not your old color, and you're not the colors Dean tried to make you. The trick is finding out what color you are now."

"I don't know if I can."

"Sure you can. And finding out could be fun," Samantha promised.

Fun?

That's not exactly the word Carly would use.

Somehow she'd do it. She'd get through January. She'd

study for her boards, do her service hours, plan the PTA's Valentine Dance, and start interviewing for a job. Working as a graduate nurse at the hospital was good, but she wasn't sure if it was where she wanted to build her career. So, she needed to figure out what sort of nursing she wanted to practice, and what color she was now.

Carly Lewis, the teenage college student, was long gone.

Carly Lewis, a perfect lawyer's wife, was gone as well.

Carly Lewis, single mother and nurse…she was just waiting to be discovered.

Chapter Two

On Monday, Carly headed downtown to the police department. She parked on Perry Square near the back of City Hall. The streets were actually clear and dry, though there were still huge piles of wet, sticky snow everywhere. It clung to the trees, weighing down their branches. The Christmas lights that the city strung in the park's trees each holiday season stuck out from under the snow at odd angles. It might have made her pause to enjoy the pretty two-block park in the center of town if she hadn't been on her way to meet with a cop.

Carly pulled her coat tighter as she walked from the Square to the rear entrance of the building. She had flashbacks to the night the young officer had brought her in. He'd been very sympathetic, but he'd also been young enough that it felt as if she was being taken in by Opie rather than Sheriff Taylor. The kid was so young he probably didn't even know who Opie and Sheriff Taylor were.

The thought was a depressing one.

She glanced at the paper the judge had given her. She was to meet with the Communication and Community Outreach Officer.

She walked through the automatic doors, then through a second set. Up the hall and to the left were doors with an Erie Bureau of Police sign hanging above it.

She unwound her scarf, but left her coat buttoned.

A cop who reached out to the community as part of his job description—he had to be nice, she assured herself. Fair and just, of course, but also nice.

Taking a deep breath, she went to the small reception room. There were a couple of chairs, a few pictures of police officers on the wall and a huge window straight across from her, with a door to the right.

Carly walked up to the glass. There was a pass-through hole at the bottom, and a metal speaker area that was probably level with most people's mouths. But Carly had to stand on tiptoe to get her mouth even close to it. "Excuse me," she said.

A woman wearing civilian clothes rather than a police uniform was working at a desk near the glass. She looked up. "Yes?"

"I have an appointment with the Communication and Community Outreach Officer. I'm Carly Lewis. It's about the safety program."

"Let me tell Chuck you're here."

A guy named Chuck was probably nice. A small bit of relief seemed to calm her nervous stomach, and Carly unbuttoned her coat.

The door next to the window opened. "Carly Lewis?" a tall, uniformed officer asked. He had very short brown hair. Shorter than hers. Not quite a buzz cut, but military-looking. Familiar-looking.

Very familiar.

It felt as if she was taking an absurdly long time to make the connection, but she was pretty sure only a moment had gone by before she had it. "You? You're the Communication and Community Outreach Officer? "

She recognized him from the day of her accidental arsonage, as well as from the judge's courtroom.

"Ah, Mrs. Lewis, you remember."

She snorted. "Like I could forget. You were that first officer on the scene. The one who doesn't get out of the office much any more. The one who's second language is sarcasm."

"My mother always says, if you have a gift, use it. And I was just filling in until the patrol guys finished up at an accident scene." He held the door open wide. "So, do you want to come into my office and I'll give you our schedule for the Safety Awareness Program?"

"Do I have a choice?" She went through the door into another hall, then waited while he walked ahead and led the way to his office.

"Certainly you have a choice. So many of our perps don't seem to understand that. They can choose to do the right thing, or not. In this case, you can choose to participate in the program, or I can call Andy and tell him you'd rather not fulfill your community service."

"Andy?" She couldn't remember having met an Andy here.

He paused, and turned around to face her. "Anderson Bradley. Judge Bradley."

She had to crane her neck in order to look the lieutenant in the eye. "You call the judge Andy?"

He started walking down the hall again, and without turning around, said over his shoulder, "My brother-in-law."

Carly shook her head. She was going to spend the next month working with the judge's brother-in-law? Great. Just great.

The lieutenant opened the door to a small cubby of an

office where there were piles of paper littering a desk. The walls were bare. There was a bookcase with binders and books jammed in it helter-skelter. He didn't seem to mind that his office was a mess.

Carly could think of a number of ways to make the small space more attractive and certainly more user-friendly. But she was out of the office redecorating business permanently, so she didn't say anything.

"Have a seat." He nodded at one of the two functional but uncomfortable looking folding chairs in the room. "So, Andy said you're coming to the Safety Awareness Program. I've got a schedule—which schools, which days."

He dug through the pile of papers on his right and miraculously produced a folder, which he promptly handed over to her. "I know Andy said you should talk about fire safety. He's warped. That's the sort of thing that would appeal to him. We're dealing with middle-school kids, not kindergarten ones. So, you're welcome to mention fire safety, if you like. But we'd hoped that since you're a nurse, you might consider manning our health booth. Last year, our health booth consisted of a few pamphlets the kids could help themselves to. I thought—we thought—that maybe a live person there would be beneficial."

"I've got a nursing degree, but I haven't passed my boards yet." She didn't want the lieutenant coming after her for not being forthright.

"You've got more knowledge than any of us do."

She glanced at the folder. There was a list with six dates and the corresponding schools. "Nine to two?"

"Some might end early, but yeah, mainly."

"Fine. I'll be there. Is there anything else, Lieutenant?"

"No, I don't think so. But here—" he reached into the pocket of his uniform shirt and took out a card and handed it to her "—if you're running late, or have any problems, call me."

"There won't be anything I can't handle. I'll be there on time, sir."

"Have I done something to offend you?"

Carly couldn't get past the memory of this man standing next to her at her fire. Well, fires. He'd been so smug, so superior while watching the mess she'd created. And she'd been crying.

That was the worst of it—he'd seen her cry.

"No, of course there's nothing wrong. I mean, I was humiliated when I caught my husband cheating, and the whole fire and charges, that's been even more embarrassing. Then, rather than the judge accepting my plea bargain, I get your brother-in-law whose warped sense of justice requires I add one more thing—no I take that back, six more things—onto my already tight-to-the-point-of-exploding schedule. And here you are again, giving me that insincere I'd-never-set-the-neighborhood-on-fire smile. So, no, officer, nothing's wrong. I'll be at each school promptly at nine, and I'll stay until two. While I'm there, I'll talk to the kids about everything from fire safety to good tooth-brushing habits."

"Listen, this wasn't my idea." He rubbed the palm of his hand against his buzz-cut.

She sighed. She was being unfair. It's just that with everyone else—including Samantha and Michelle—she could play off the whole accidental-arson thing as if it didn't bother her.

But this man, through no fault of his own, had witnessed her embarrassment. He'd seen her tears. He knew that the changes mattered to her. She could be as flippant as she wanted to and pretend she was tough, but he knew better. And that made her feel exposed—vulnerable. She didn't like these feelings, so she was going to ignore them. She'd do her best to remain totally professional and aloof around him.

"You're right. It wasn't your idea. And it wasn't mine. However, we're both stuck with it, so we'll make the best of it. I'll see you—" she glanced in the file "—a week from tomorrow. If I need to know or do anything more than what you've indicated in this folder, call me."

"You didn't give me your number."

"I was arrested, remember? I'm sure you have it on file." And with that, she waltzed out of the room with as much dignity as she could muster.

It was going to be a very long January.

She had to study for her boards, work, organize the Valentine's dance for the Social Planning Committee and now this. Not to mention the kids. She'd spent so long looking forward to the new year. To starting over.

New Year's Eve wasn't until Wednesday, and she was already wishing it was February.

CHUCK WATCHED CARLY Lewis…strut?

Stalk?

No, flounce.

Yes, Carly Lewis flounced from his office, the file grasped a little too tightly. He was going to kill Andy. The last thing he needed was a pissed off firebug *helping* him with the safety program.

His phone rang, and he picked it up without checking the caller ID. "Lieutenant Jefferson, Communication and Community Outreach."

He hated that his title was so long. He'd lobbied for something shorter. Mouthpiece of the Station, for instance. The Deputy Chief had nixed it.

"Chuck, it's Mom."

"Oh." Knowing that sounded less than enthusiastic, he quickly added, "Always good to hear from you, Mom."

His mother snorted. "Christmas is over. You don't have to try and be nice in order to secure a good gift."

"Mom, really, can't a son just be happy to hear from his mother?" He swung his chair around so he could look out the window that faced snow-covered Perry Square.

Cars lined the curb of the two-block park. He wondered which one, if any, was Carly's.

"Yes, I'm sure some sons are happy to hear from their mothers, but Charles, darling, you're not one. At least you won't be when I tell you that you're expected at dinner this weekend. I know it's only Monday," she assured him hastily. "But I also know if I don't give you plenty of notice, you'll be 'too busy' to come. And when I say 'too busy' I'm air-quoting it as a visual indication that I'm being sarcastic. I wasn't sure you heard the sarcasm over the phone."

"I heard it." It didn't take anyone overly astute to recognize his mother's sarcasm. His mom didn't do subtle well, probably because she didn't even try.

"See, you're such a smart boy. You must get it from your very intelligent mother, who's putting you on notice—dinner on Sunday."

He might as well start laying the groundwork for skipping out last-minute. "I'll be there if I can, but you know what my job's like."

His mother scoffed. "I know that for the first time since you started working as a cop, you're on a weekdays, nine-to-five schedule. No more swing shifts, no more weekends, which means you're able to come to dinner on Sundays. It's your New Year's resolution. Having a meal with your family each Sunday."

"I thought *I* was supposed to make my resolution." He scanned the sidewalk, looking for Carly Lewis.

"Have you made any resolutions?" his mom countered.

"New Year's Eve isn't for a few days, I have time."

"You also have time to start the new year off with weekly family dinners. Five o'clock on Sunday. If you're not there, I'll have Andy swear out a contempt of court against you."

"Andy's coming?"

The moment the words left his mouth he realized how they sounded, but he didn't have time to take them back because his mother answered immediately. He could hear the pain in her voice. "Andy's family. No matter what, he'll always be family, so of course he's coming."

As if shaking off the vulnerability he'd heard in her words, she added in her most bossy-mom voice, "And so are you. Don't forget. Five."

"I—"

"Oh, and I should mention that if you're dating someone, she's welcome as well. You know me, there's always twice as much food as we need."

There she was.

Carly.

The public entrance to the police station was on the other side of the building. Which meant she'd gone out the back and had to walk the length of the block to get to her car. He watched, waiting to see which vehicle she approached. But rather than going to one of the cars, she headed into the park, toward the gazebo.

When he didn't say anything, his mother added, "Charles, it's time for you to settle down. It's been a long time since Ami."

"I've dated since Ami," he answered by rote. His concentration was on Carly. What was she doing?

"But no one for very long. Nothing serious. You haven't dated anyone long enough to come meet your mother. Not since Ami."

He wished his mother would stop saying his ex's name. "Mom, I'm an adult."

"And I'm your mother. I want you to be happy. You need a good woman in your life. And I've decided that my New Year's resolution is going to be finding you one."

That was just what he needed. His mother on a matchmaking mission. "I don't need my mother finding me dates."

"Fine, then bring your own."

"Mom—"

"I'm serious, Charles. You find a woman to date, or I'll find one for you. And if you find one between now and Sunday, bring her to dinner."

He didn't say anything because for the life of him, he couldn't think of anything to say. He was the voice of the police department, both on camera and at community events like the Safety Awareness Program.

He was the one they shoved in front of the reporters whenever they came to cover a story. The Chief had told him he got the job because he was articulate and quick on his feet. So, why was it his mother could reduce him to an inarticulate blob?

"Charles, did you hear me?"

"I heard you, Mom. And I'll see you Sunday. Gotta go." He hung up and reminded himself that in the future he should always, always check the caller ID. How hard was that to remember?

The idea of a Sunday dinner at his parents' didn't appeal. It wasn't that he didn't love his family and didn't like spending time with them. It's just that Sunday dinners should include everyone, and because they no longer did, it just seemed to emphasize what was missing. Who was missing.

Chuck shook his head. He wasn't going to think about what was missing. His mom was right, they had to find a way to put themselves back together.

So Chuck would go to dinner and make nice for a couple hours.

He was welcome to bring a date, his mom had said.

It had been a while since he broke up with his last girl-friend, Patty. She was nice enough and they'd gotten along fine, but there was no spark. No chemisty.

Besides, he'd seen too many relationships fail. Hell, he'd had what he thought was a long-term relationship with Ami when he'd joined the department at twenty-three. And she hadn't lasted a year. She hated the fact he worked swing shifts, and had odd days off.

But now his mother had vowed to find him a woman… unless he found one himself.

He just needed a body.

A female body.

Not necessarily someone he was dating, just someone to come to a dinner and get his mom off his back for a while.

As he reflected on his mother's New Year's resolution for him, he still watched across the street. What the hell was Carly doing?

She'd walked to the gazebo in the middle of the park and was kneeling by a homeless guy who was sitting on the steps.

Chuck was up, out of his chair, and hurrying through the private door that opened directly onto South Park Row and the Square.

What on earth was the crazy woman thinking approaching a stranger? Obviously, thinking wasn't her strongest suit. After all she did torch her neighborhood. Okay, accidentally, but still…

He was so annoyed he hardly took note of the cold wind blowing in off the lake or the fact that he was freezing because he hadn't paused to put a coat on. He caught Carly just as she was walking away from the guy toward the line of parked cars. "What were you thinking?"

She stopped short, looked up and made a face as if she'd bitten into a lemon. "Pardon?"

"I asked what were you thinking? You don't just go talk to strangers in the park."

"And if I said he wasn't a stranger?" Her arms crossed, clutching the file to her chest as she tapped her foot.

Chuck didn't need any major insight to realize she was annoyed. That didn't faze him in the least. He was annoyed, too. And he'd match his annoyance to hers any day. "I'd say he still doesn't look like a very savory character."

"And I'd say mind your own business. Your crazy brother-in-law said I had to help with your safety thing, and I will, but that's where our relationship ends. And it so happens that I was finishing my rotation at the ER last month when Mr. Deever came in. I wanted to say hi and see how he was doing, not that it is in any way your business, and even if it were, I still wouldn't permit you to take that tone with me. Save the cop tone for cop business."

"If you'd been assaulted in the park, it would have been cop business."

"It's broad daylight, no one was assaulting me but you." She looked meaningfully at her arm.

Chuck hadn't realized he'd grabbed her arm. He dropped his hand immediately. "Sorry. You scared me."

"What, a woman who accidentally burns down a few sheds

becomes such a big danger to herself and the community that you have to worry?"

"I—" What was it about this woman? She was turning him into a blathering idiot, and to date, the only other woman with that capability was his mother.

An idea started to form.

It was a crazy thought—one he'd hesitate to mention to any other woman but Carly, who'd already shown that she did crazy quite well. "I have an idea."

Carly shook her head. "Men and kids…it's never a good thing when either has an idea."

"You see, I need a date."

"Whoa, there, boy. That's not going to happen. Ever. Never." She paused a moment, then added, "And if that wasn't clear enough, no. Absolutely not. I've already decided I'll never marry again, but I haven't ruled out dating. However, I'm officially ruling out dating you. I have made a list of what I'm looking for in a man I date, though. And you don't possess any of the qualities I'd want."

Chuck wished he'd grabbed his coat. It was freezing outside, but it was Carly's attitude that was truly arctic.

He should take her rather emphatic no and go in. Instead, he found himself asking, "Such as?"

"If I date, I'd want a quiet man. One who wouldn't tell me what I should or shouldn't do. One who would allow me to stand on my own two feet because I guarantee that I won't be relying on a man ever again. Someone compatible. Nice even. One who doesn't mind kids and pets."

Just turn and walk away, he told himself, and instead asked, "And how do you know I'm not that man?"

"May I remind you that we've only met on two occasions, and still you felt you had the right to come running and be sure I wasn't assaulted by a patient? That whole wouldn't-tell-me-what-I-should-and-shouldn't-do? You blew that. And the quiet thing? I'll confess, I don't see that in you either."

"Maybe I like kids and pets, and some people think I'm nice." He wasn't sure why he was pushing. He absolutely didn't want to date this woman for real. She was all bristles and snarls. He liked softer women.

Carly Lewis was all edges.

She snorted at his I'm-nice statement. That sort of raised his hackles. "Listen, I simply thought it might be a win-win situation."

"Who'd win what?" she asked.

"I'd come to Sunday dinner with a woman in tow, so my mom wouldn't begin her New Year's resolution campaign and start fixing me up."

"Okay there's a win for you, but I don't see one for me. So, no thanks." She shook her head and started walking toward the cars.

Chuck followed her. "I'd say a nice meal that you don't have to cook—Mom's a good cook."

She glanced behind her and shook her head again. "I can get take-out just as easy if I don't want to cook."

The head-shaking thing was starting to get to him. He wanted to tell her if she continued shaking it that hard she was going to shake her few remaining brain cells loose, but he didn't think that would endear him to her, so he bit his tongue. "But that wasn't my big win for you. Your big win would be the fact that Andy will be there. And having spent the last few minutes in your company, I can only imagine how hard it was for you to bite your tongue in his courtroom. And you *had* to bite it because he's the judge. But at my mother's table, you're both guests. You'd have free rein to make his life—well at least his dinner—miserable."

That made her stop. As she turned to face him, there was a twinkle in her dark-brown eyes that said she rather liked the idea. "And you'd be on my side? No threats to haul me off to jail or anything?"

"If you're on my side and therefore against my mother as my own personal matchmaker, then you've got an ally against Andy." His brother-in-law was his best friend, but he still owed Andy for making sure the picture of him dressed up as a cowboy found it's way onto the police department's bulletin board. Chuck still got an occasional "yippee" from the guys. He could see that Carly was wavering, so he threw in, "And, of course, your kids are welcome, too."

"They're with their father next weekend." Her frown spoke volumes.

"Is there a problem with him and the kids? I could—"

"No, nothing like that." This time she shook her head softly. "It's just…the secretary he was boffing on my couch?"

How on earth could he forget that particular story? He nodded.

"She's moved in with him. So she's there on the weekends he has the kids. I've got a friend who's actually friendly with her ex's new girlfriend, and I've tried to emulate her and be forgiving. I've tried to be adult about it. But I've found I'm not able to be. I put on a good front for the kids, though. They don't need to feel caught in the middle. But honestly, I don't think the fire purged all of my bitterness as I'd intended. Maybe the fact I was worried about burning down the neighborhood overtook its purging effect."

"I don't know anyone who'd recover completely from something like that," Chuck assured her. "You're a good mom not putting the kids in the middle."

"You sound surprised."

Chuck was pretty sure he had the beginning of frostbite on his hands. He tried to keep his teeth from chattering as he answered, "In my line of work, I've found most divorced couples spend so much time hating each other they rarely have time to spare a thought for their kids and what the animosity is doing to them."

Carly cocked her head to the side, studying him. She let out a long, low whistle. "Lieutenant, you are officially even more jaded than me."

He didn't take offense because she was right. Instead, while she was looking less defensive, he asked, "So, dinner on Sunday at five?"

No head shaking this time…she nodded instead. "I have to be home by nine when my ex drops off the kids."

"That's a yes?"

"Good that you're in charge of PR and not a detective if that's the best you can do. Yes, it's a yes, Lieutenant. Just don't get any ideas that this is more than me taking advantage of an opportunity to needle 'Andy—'" she used his nickname for his brother-in-law with obvious delight "—without being tossed in jail for contempt."

He held up his hand and made a scout sign. "I swear, no illusions of us liking each other. And it might be best if you started calling me Chuck instead of Lieutenant. I'll pick you up at four-thirty."

"Fine, *Chuck*." She started walking toward the row of cars lining the Square and moved toward a van.

It was a very mommish vehicle. If he'd chosen, he'd have said Carly drove a Jeep. Tough, able to go off-road, take a beating and still get her where she wanted to go. Yet, there she was getting in a van. A soft, mommish van.

"Hey, I need an address," he called before she got in.

"You've got that on file, too," she repeated. "I'm sure you'll figure it out."

He watched her exit her parking space and head around the Square. He would very definitely figure it out.

When he heard Andy's claim in the courtroom, Chuck had been less than enthusiastic. But after today, the January Safety Awareness Program was looking to be a lot more interesting than he'd anticipated.

January

"SAMANTHA, I HAVE NO idea why I said yes," Carly said on Friday as she trailed after Samantha from examination room to examination room.

She'd seen healthy kids who'd come in for immunizations and check-ups, kids with flu, kids with scrapes, breaks and the occasional mystery rash. It was so nice of Dr. Jackson to let her shadow Samantha today. But rather than concentrating on what nursing in a pediatric practice was like, all she could think about was her dinner with Chuck's family in two days.

Samantha ignored Carly's rhetorical question as she stood at a nurses' station and updated the chart from the last patient, five-year-old Jessie, who'd come in with a BB in her ear. "Are the kids going with you? They could come have dinner at my place, if you'd like."

"They'll be at their dad's. I take them over right after school tonight, and he'll bring them back Sunday night by nine. So they're no problem."

"Well, then, there you go." Samantha went back to work on the file. "You're single, the kids are accounted for. There was absolutely no reason not to say yes."

"Except I don't like Chuck at all. It's not a real date, he

made that clear, and sure, I'm relieved, because he's nothing like the man I'll date when I start to date again."

Samantha paused and looked up. "You've given this some thought."

"Sure. When I date again—and despite the fact it doesn't sound the least bit appealing right now, I suspect it will again someday—when that day comes, I want someone who's the antithesis of Dean. Loyal, quiet. Someone who doesn't mind my independence, and is independent himself. The lieutenant is anything but quiet, and he's bossy. You should have seen his office. It almost made Sean's room look neat, and that's hard to do."

"Well, see, you're just a cover. No worries. A free meal, some adult conversation. It's win-win. And of course, there's the chance to needle the judge."

Carly grinned at the thought. "Yeah, there is that."

"So relax." Samantha deposited the updated file in a basket, and grabbed the next one. "I'm sure you're right and it's nothing."

"Okay, you're right." She felt better. More centered. Samantha was like that. She mothered everyone, and Carly wouldn't have admitted it out loud, but she'd needed that today. It was at a moment like this that losing her parents kicked her all over again, even after all these years.

"So, about the Valentine's dance?" Samantha said, changing the subject. "How's that coming? Did you get a band or DJ? Michelle and I are here to offer whatever help you need."

"I figured we'd just set up an iPod station with speakers all over. I know that Sean and his buddies did something like that for a party and the kids loved doing their own music."

"Kids?"

Carly nodded. "At the dance."

"Carly, did you look at the file Michelle gave you?"

"Not yet. I mean, with finals, graduation, work and interning, not to mention my brush with the law, I haven't had much time. It was on my list for this week. It's barely January and I've got until February. How hard can it be? You and Michelle got the two hardest events."

"Carly, the dance isn't for the kids. It's for the adults. All the parents of current students and alumni of the school. Pretty much anyone who will pay for the ticket. A fund-raiser that's practically a mini-reunion. If you'd read the file, you'd have seen that the PTA voted to change it last year."

"But…I mean…" Last year was a haze. She'd been so unbelievably busy and missed a lot of meetings. "I must have missed that discussion and vote last year."

Missing PTA meetings was definitely something she'd avoid in the future. Nothing good ever came from missing a PTA meeting. She had the folder Michelle had given her, but she'd only given it a cursory glance because she knew she couldn't really work on the dance until January, and hadn't anticipated it being a big deal.

"You're sure about the adult thing?" she asked, weakly.

"Positive."

"Seriously, I want to know what I've done in my past to anger the universe. I am a woman who doesn't believe in romance, but I figured the dance wasn't a problem because it was for the kids. I'd bring in a sound system for them, throw up a few paper streamers, and have some snacks on hand, and I'd be done. But adults? Happy couples all over the place dancing and making googly Valentine eyes at each other? I'm going to hurl worse than that kid in Exam Two."

"Michelle and I will help," Samantha promised.

Carly knew that Samantha meant her offer, but rather than

just accepting or declining she groused. "You and Michelle will be two of the worst—"

"Googly-eyed couples?" Samantha's grin said she wasn't insulted in the least.

"Yeah."

"Sorry." Samantha didn't look the least bit apologetic, either.

"Don't get me wrong," Carly assured her. "I'm happy for you and Harry and for Michelle and Daniel, but…" She shook her head. "A Valentine's dance for adults, and dinner with my warden and the judge who sentenced me. My life continues its downhill spiral."

"Well, the good news is you've got nowhere to go but up."

Carly snorted. Samantha had been a unending font of optimism since they'd met. She claimed it was all because of some book, but Carly suspected that Samantha was at heart a Pollyanna.

If there was an antithesis of Pollyanna, that's what Carly was.

Planning an adult Valentine's dance was a lot different than planning something for kids. What an idiot to not have known that this was a grown-up affair and fund-raiser?

An adult Valentine's dance.

She'd suspected that the universe hated her since the moment she'd found her husband with his secretary.

Now she was sure.

Chapter Three

Chuck kicked the snow off his boots as he walked up the steps to Carly's porch and knocked on the door of the small, story-and-a-half bungalow on Erie's east side that Sunday.

As a cop he had a feel for most neighborhoods. This one was soundly middle-class. Quiet for the most part. The kind of place where the police were usually called out for nothing more serious than barking dogs or loud parties. It was a great neighborhood for raising a family.

Carly opened the door and frowned. "You found me."

"Wow, lucky thing I have a healthy ego, otherwise that greeting might have done some damage."

"I don't see any chance of any long-term damage to your ego." She opened the door a little wider and let him into a very bright foyer. Not bright because of any out-of-character sunshine. Erie was overcast more often than not this time of year. And today was a more-often day.

No, it was bright because of the cacophony of color. Bright-yellow walls. A coat rack that had the whole array of crayon colors. Red. Blue. Green. Orange. Down one side of the door was a collection of nicely framed prints of impressionist art, and down the other side was a huge mirror that reflected the foyer back on itself.

The small entryway might have been too much in another house, but because it was Carly's, it seemed appropriate. Inviting even—though he doubted she'd meant any invitation for him. Especially given her you've-got-a-big-ego comments.

"Ouch again. This is going to be an interesting night." Hopefully interesting enough to get his mother to forget his single status.

"Do you want to cancel?" There was a tone to her voice that said his wanting to cancel wouldn't be the worst news she'd ever received.

"No," he said. Her face fell, so he asked, "Do you?"

Rather than answer, she countered with, "This plan of yours doesn't sound very—I don't know—coply. I mean, you guys are supposed to be brave and tough. Taking a decoy date because you're scared of your mother smacks of something less than that."

"Listen, I've broken up fights, arrested drug dealers, I've dealt with more domestics than I can count. None of them scare me. I'm cautious, but not frightened. But my mother on a mission? There's no stopping that. It's an act of nature, ready to run over whoever's in its path. Namely, me."

His mom used to divide her attention between him and Julia, his sister. Thinking of his sister's passing robbed him of the fun of needling Carly. He missed Julia, dammit. He forced himself to put the sad thoughts away and pointed out, "And don't forget, you can pick on Andy."

"There is that. And if I call him Andy, it will annoy him?"

"Guaranteed. Everyone and their brother calls him Anderson, or Your Honor. My sister started calling him Andy when they dated. She said it kept him humble."

Carly grinned. "Humbling *Andy* is a huge draw for this evening. Okay, let me get my coat."

She slid her coat off the hook, put it on without bothering to button it. He thought about telling her she should—it couldn't be more than twenty degrees out—but he didn't imagine that would go over well, so he kept silent.

She grabbed her purse, held the door open for him followed him, out and slammed the door behind her. Carly turned and checked the door handle was locked. For some reason, that gave him comfort.

"Let's go then. Mom and Dad don't live far from here."

Carly was quiet on the ride over. That suited Chuck just fine. He was still trying to figure out why he hadn't let her change her mind about tonight. He probably should have. He'd had second thoughts about his dinner invitation ever since he'd offered it. But when the opportunity came to back out, he'd talked her into coming instead.

It wasn't just that her being there would get his mom off his back. There was something about Carly that spoke to him. She lived life in a big, bold way, just like the colors of her foyer.

Burning the couch to purge her past. He'd laughed with the guys over it, but in private he'd sort of admired the act. There were times in his past he wished he could purge. Unfortunately, the city frowned on its officers torching couches, and he didn't think that particular method would work for him anyway.

He pulled up in front of his parents Glenwood Hills tudor-style home. Anderson's truck was already in the drive. "We're here. And it looks like Andy's here as well."

"Oh, good."

Carly's happiness didn't bode well for his brother-in-law. "Come on. We can talk about the program as well. The first one's Tuesday."

He led her onto the porch.

"I didn't forget, Lieutenant. I'll be there."

"Chuck. This would probably work better if you called me Chuck." He opened the front door. "Hey, Mom, I'm here. You might want to set another plate."

His mom hurried out of the kitchen and spied Carly. "You brought someone. A woman someone."

"You told me to. Mom, this is Carly, Carly, my mother, Linda Jefferson."

"Pleased to meet you, ma'am. And it's apparent Chuck didn't tell you I was coming. Let me apologize for crashing your family dinner." Carly shot Chuck a look that said the ride home might be peppered with recriminations.

"No apologies, dear. I did tell him to bring someone any time, so this is a pleasant surprise. Here, let me take your coat for you. My son obviously has no manners." Linda hung Carly's coat in the closet and said, "There, now you just make yourself at home."

"Can I help you with anything?"

His mother's face lit up. "Oh, that would be lovely. It's been a long time since I had another woman help me in the kitchen. I tried to be a woman's libber and make sure my son could navigate the difficult world of preparing food. But the boy never could master anything, not even a box of macaroni and cheese. I'm such a failure."

It was an old complaint, one that Chuck had long since learned to placate. "Ah, but if I'd learned to cook for myself, I wouldn't drop in nearly as often to bum food off you and you'd miss me."

"He's right," his mom stage-whispered to Carly. "Now, you come along with me. Chuck, your Dad and Anderson are in the family room watching a NASCAR race."

"You sure you don't mind?" he asked Carly.

She smiled. "I'm fine."

Chuck was nervous. The plan had not been to have his mother bond with Carly. This might have been a bad idea.

He found his dad and Anderson cheering on their personal drivers. "Jeff can *so* take Tony in his Toyota," his dad said loudly.

Chuck knew the Jeff in question was Jeff Burton, number thirty-one. He drove a Chevy, and Timothy August Jefferson had always been a GM guy.

Chuck was pretty sure Anderson had chosen to cheer for someone who was not only not Jeff Burton, but also not on the Chevy team. Tony Stewart, number twenty, fit the bill. And Anderson's devotion to Tony was a continued thorn in Chuck's father's side.

"Hey, Chuck," his dad said without looking up. "Your mom's in the kitchen. Sit down and watch. It's Daytona."

Chuck sat down. "I thought the races started in February."

"It's a repeat," his father said, with that certain, how-can-he-be-a-son-of-mine-and-not-realize-that? inflection in his voice. "They show old races on cable."

"Seriously, I knew about Dad's addiction, but you too, Andy?"

"Not addicted, just enthusiastic. And lay off the Andys, Chuck. Show a little respect."

Today was going to be fun. Even though he knew bringing Carly here might not have been his brightest idea—images of his mom and Carly bonding in the kitchen flashed through his mind—that's why he'd done it anyway.

He grinned at his brother-in-law. "I do respect you and re-spectfully decline to feed that overinflated ego of yours, so you're Andy."

Anderson sighed. "You Jeffersons have always been an in-corrigible lot."

"Hey," his dad complained. "How did I get lumped into that?"

"By virtue of contributing half this one's DNA." Anderson jerked his head in Chuck's direction.

His dad laughed. "Gee, one night of passion and—"

Nothing in Chuck wanted to hear anything about his parents being associated with the word *passion*. "TMI, Dad, TMI."

"Did I hear a woman's voice?" Anderson asked.

"You did." To warn Anderson, or not to warn Anderson? Chuck hadn't decided when his mother called, "Hit Pause on your race, Tim, and come out to dinner."

"I thought we'd just eat in here," his father hollered back, more to goad his wife than for any other reason, Chuck was sure.

She didn't even bother to respond.

"Come on, boys." Tim hit the Pause button on the DVR. "Time for our first traditional weekly Sunday dinner."

"Let's go meet Chuck's new woman. Bet I can scare her off with stories," Anderson said with glee—very unjudge-like glee.

He stopped in the dining-room doorway. Chuck knew Anderson had spotted Carly even before his brother-in-law turned and asked, "Her?"

Chuck nodded, and looping an arm over Anderson's shoulder, led the very reluctant judge into the dining room.

Carly gave a little wave. *"Andy,"* she practically crooned, leaving a very pregnant pause that made the emphasis on his nickname even more pronounced, "it's so good to see you again outside the courtroom. I think the pink polo shirt is way closer to your color than that awful black robe."

Chuck noticed that Anderson looked down on his not-quite pink—it was more salmon—polo shirt and he could swear his brother-in-law, who spent his days working with hardened criminals blushed as he stammered out, "Wh-what are you doing here?" in a definitely less-than-friendly manner.

"Anderson Bradley," Chuck's mother scolded, "I won't have you use that voice with my guests. You save it for the criminals in your court."

Anderson pointed at Carly. "She *was* one of the criminals in my court just last week." He shot her a got-ya look.

"Now, Andy…" Carly started in a hurt tone, then stopped abruptly, as if going on was too hard.

Chuck would have testified in court that the tears pooling in her eyes were real. At least, he would have until she shot him a private wink.

No one said anything. The silence dragged out to an uncomfortable length until Chuck finally said, "There were extenuating circumstances. Let's start dinner and I'm sure Carly will tell you all about it, Mom."

Chuck sat next to Carly who whispered, "Thanks," as the food was passed from person to person.

He could tell she was warming up for a full-blown performance. And though he'd not spent much time with her, he was pretty sure it would be Oscar-worthy.

"So, Carly, dear, what happened?" his mom asked.

"Well, Mrs. Jefferson, it's not a short story by any means." She took a spoonful of potatoes.

"Oh, sweetie, we have time. But I saw you tear up. If it's too difficult—"

"No. Though before I tell you, I need you to understand I'm not a bad person."

Oh, yeah, an Oscar *and* an Emmy. Maybe even a People's Choice Award…at least if he was the person voting and not Anderson.

"You see, Mrs. Jefferson, it all started when I redecorated my then-husband's office. I really worked at it. I mean, everything coordinated and looked so very lawyerly. My ex insisted on presenting the right impression, so the more lawyerly it looked, the better. My only sticking point was finding the right couch. I shopped for months, but I finally found it. Oh, ma'am, it was a thing to behold. That couch didn't just say, it screamed, be confident in me I can win your case."

"That's a very big statement for a couch to be making." Anderson speared a piece of his meat loaf with far more force than necessary.

"As a judge who puts on a robe as a visual clue that he's in charge—and if that fails, threatens people with contempt of court and all manner of not-so-nice things—I'm sure you realize that sometimes a man needs the illusion of power in order to boost his very fragile manly ego."

"Ouch," Chuck muttered.

He could tell that Carly almost lost it then and smiled, but she held her features in their pained expression, then dabbed at her eyes with her napkin to cover her momentary look of enjoyment.

"Anyway," she continued as she set the napkin on her lap. "I went to his office after hours to celebrate the new decor and I found—I found—I found him already celebrating on *my* couch…celebrating with his secretary, if you get my meaning."

"How clichéd," Mrs. Jefferson said and shot all three males at the table a dirty look.

Carly nodded, happy to have an ally. "That's what I've been saying. I mean, if a guy's going to cheat, seriously, you'd think he could find someone less ordinary. Although, I guess the fact that I divorced him after I found him with her, is rather clichéd as well. I fought for and won that couch in the settlement. But Mrs. Jefferson, I was so angry and bitter."

"I would be, too, dear." And she shot her husband another dirty look.

Chuck watched his father's roll stop halfway to his mouth as he asked, "Hey, why am I in trouble? Innocent bystander here."

"You're male," his mother said.

CARLY WAS PRETTY SURE she was going to like Chuck's mom. Warming up to her story, Carly continued, "I have two wonderful kids, and I will be forced to see my ex until they're grown. After that, too. Weddings, grandbabies and the like. So, I needed to rid myself that bitterness so I could move on and forge a more amicable relationship with the cheating, clichéd-secretary-boffing scum of an ex. And I did. When he brought the couch to the house, I had him set it in the backyard, and then I doused it with gas and lit it on fire. I mean, really, I would never have been able to sit on it…not after what I saw."

"I don't blame you," Mrs. Jefferson assured her.

"The problem is, my son and my ex, who'd carried the couch into the backyard, had set it very close to my shed— which caught on fire. And my shed is very close to the neighbor's—which also caught on fire."

"Oh, dear." Mrs. Jefferson reached over and patted Carly's hand.

"And that's when Chuck here came to arrest me."

"Charles August Jefferson, you arrested her?" Mrs. Jefferson smacked his hand.

"Hey, I didn't arrest her, I was out doing a neighborhood watch meeting, and I'd just left when I heard the call. I was close, so I checked it out and merely waited until one of the street guys came and took her in."

"The young officer who Chuck handed me over to was

very kind. He seemed to feel for my plight, unlike your son who smirked at me while we waited."

Chuck's mom smacked his hand again. "I raised you better than that, Charles."

"Uh-oh, you're in trouble when she calls you Charles, Charles," Anderson said.

"I've forgiven Chuck, ma'am. He's been very sweet." Chuck frowned as she used the word *sweet*. It wasn't precisely the truth, but this was his mom and a smart woman knows that you don't win a mother over by trash-talking her son. And Carly was smart.

"But Andy there," she said slowly, "he's harder to forgive, though I'm trying. I really wanted to be done with bitter recriminations. That's what the fire was all about. It would be a shame to suffer with them still after everything that happened."

"And Andy was mean to you?"

Carly glanced over and saw the judge grimace as Mrs. Jefferson used his nickname.

"Yes. A.D.A. Kelly and my lawyer had a lovely plea agreement all worked out, but when we got in front of Judge Andy here, he refused to accept it. So now, in addition to restitution—which I made right after the fire, on my own—I have to do community service with Chuck. And Mrs. Jefferson, I'm a single mom, balancing work and studying for my nursing boards, and planning a Valentine's dance for my kids' school—which I thought was just for the kids, but it turns out it's for adults, and you know that's going to take a lot more planning. You can throw a bag of chips at kids and they're happy. But adults are more discriminating in their tastes. So it's going to be work. And now Andy added more onto that. There are days I can't find time to eat, which makes today's meal all that much nicer."

For emphasis, she took a large bite of her potatoes.

"Both of you boys, I'm so ashamed." Mrs. Jefferson scooped another spoonful of potatoes on Carly's plate. "You're such a tiny little thing as it is. You just eat up, dear." Then she scowled at Anderson again.

"I was an accidental arsonist, ma'am. I never meant to burn anything except that couch and all my bitter memories." Carly took a huge bite of potatoes and tried to really relish Anderson's expression. It was somewhere between annoyance and acceptance.

Speaking of annoyance, Mrs. Jefferson's annoyance with *the boys* was evident as she clucked and sympathized her way through the meal. Andy glowered at Carly, which somehow made the evening even more fun.

After dinner, Mrs. Jefferson took a load of dishes into the kitchen, and Carly started to help clear the table.

"You enjoyed that," Anderson accused. "Both of you."

Chuck shrugged, not the least bit intimidated by his brother-in-law. "Hey, I just brought a guest, like Mom instructed."

"I did enjoy it. And you did deserve it," Carly admitted with a grin, then slowly added, "Andy."

"The appropriate way to address me is Your Honor, Judge Bradley or even Anderson, since we're not in court."

Carly shrugged. "I think I prefer Andy."

"I could hold you in contempt," Anderson grumbled.

"Could he?" she asked Chuck, suddenly nervous.

Sure, taunting a judge was all fun and games until you found yourself in jail on a contempt charge. She watched court television and all those lawyer shows. She knew that judges could keep you in jail indefinitely. The idea of a questionable roommate and even more questionable bathroom accommodations made her wish she'd ignored Chuck's invitation.

"No idea if he can do that outside of court," Chuck not-so-helpfully informed her.

She knew she should apologize. She would have apologized before her divorce. She'd spent years learning how not to rock the boat under Dean's tutelage. And maybe that's why she found herself saying, "Guess I'll just have to live on the wild side, *Andy*."

"Is everything all right out there?" Mrs. Jefferson called.

"Everything's fine, Mrs. Jefferson. I was just gathering the plates while Andy here threatened me with contempt of court." She sighed her most pathetic sigh.

Mrs. Jefferson poked her head into the room. "Anderson Bradley, I won't have you passing out contempt charges willy-nilly at my Sunday dinner, do you hear me?"

"Yes, ma'am," Anderson said with a meekness Carly had never heard before.

"Fine. You boys help Carly clear the table." Mrs. Anderson stalked back into the kitchen without checking to see if the adults in the room were obeying.

"Does anyone else here feel like they are in grade school?" Anderson asked as he started gathering the serving bowls.

"Yes," Carly assured him. "I mean, I just had the most overwhelming urge to say 'neener, neener, neener,' and stick my tongue out at you."

She wasn't sure, but she thought there was the slightest twitchy upturn of Anderson's lips, as if he might want to smile. "If I *was* allowed to threaten contempt of courts in this dining room…that would probably earn one."

"The threat, or the contempt?"

"Both," he in a tone she couldn't quite interpret.

Chuck carried a stack of plates into the kitchen and Carly

started to follow him, but Anderson touched her elbow, stopping her.

"Carly, I just wanted to say, my intent wasn't to make your life more difficult. I really thought that doing some easy service hours with Chuck would be a cakewalk, and would allow me to expunge your record sooner. It will all be cleared by the end of January, rather than a year from now. It's hard to look for a job with a record."

"That's true," she said, not sure she believed his excuse.

"It is, believe me. But in court, I don't generally indulge in warm-fuzzies. I have a reputation as a hard-ass, and I'll confess that it works in my favor. So don't tell anybody, okay?"

She looked at the too-young-to-be-a-judge man, and felt a twinge of guilt. "I won't tell."

Right on cue, Chuck walked into the room. "Hey, Mom's nervous about the two of you being in here alone. And what aren't you telling, Carly?"

"No idea what you're talking about." Carly winked at Anderson, then took her stack of plates into the kitchen.

"She's an interesting one," she heard Anderson say, though she didn't hear Chuck's response.

LATER THAT NIGHT, as Chuck drove her home, she looked across the seat at him. His face was illuminated by the street lights. Lit one minute, shadowed the next.

It was a nice face.

A very nice face.

Dean's face had an aristocratic air to it. A suave sort of good looks. Handsome.

No one would say Chuck was handsome. He was…cute.

The thought made her smile. She was pretty sure Erie's own Lieutenant of Communication and Community Outreach wouldn't enjoy being described as cute. But there it was…he wasn't the least bit handsome, but he was very, very cute.

"What are you smiling about?" he asked, after a quick glance in her direction,

Although self-restraint wasn't one of Carly's gifts, she managed to practice a bit of it now. "I was just thinking."

"Carly, we haven't known each other very long, but I'm thinking your thinking is a dangerous thing."

"I've heard that before." She sighed.

He pulled up in front of her house. "I do want to thank you for helping me out tonight with my mother."

"You're welcome. I had fun." She was as surprised as Chuck looked to hear herself say those words. "Listen, I love my kids, but it's nice to have an adult conversation during a meal for a change. And I'll confess, I'm sort of looking forward to Tuesday. We haven't talked about it, but I've got a lot of information for the kids."

"Great."

"Before I get out of the car, I want to say thanks for the invitation. Needling Anderson was fun. I meant to ask where your sister was? I'd really have enjoyed meeting her."

"Sorry, Carly. I thought I'd explained." He paused, then said, very business-like, "My sister Julia died last year."

"Oh." She thought about how she'd taunted Anderson, and felt horrible. "I'm so sorry."

"We all were. She and Andy were talking about starting a family, and they thought she was pregnant. I'd never seen them both so happy. Then they found out it wasn't a pregnancy—she had uterine cancer. By the time they'd caught it, it was systemic."

Carly went from feeling bad to feeling worse. "Oh, Chuck, how awful."

"Anderson, well, he's changed since losing Julia. I don't think he's fully recovered yet."

"And then I come along and spend a family dinner picking at him." She hadn't known about Anderson Bradley's wife, but Chuck had. And Anderson had admitted he'd thrown out the plea in order to help her.

Worse and worse. She turned to Chuck. "You *let* me do that. You let me go in and spend a meal making his life even more miserable, knowing that he hadn't recovered. How could you?"

"Carly, that was the most I've heard out of Andy in the last year. Maybe he needed a challenge." Then he muttered, "And let me assure you, you're a challenge all right."

"Nice. Use me to torment a man who's obviously tormented enough without my help, then insult me. I'm going in." She opened the door, got out of the car and toward her porch.

Chuck unrolled his window and called, "I'll still see you early Tuesday morning then?"

She turned around. "You wouldn't if I had a choice, but since I don't, yeah I'll be there." She unlocked the front door and bolted inside before he had time to say goodbye. She locked the door and peeked out the window. Chuck's car didn't move for another moment, then slowly pulled away.

Wow, that had been the weirdest night of her life.

For a second in the car, she'd thought Chuck was cute.

A cute cop.

No way was she going down that path. She wasn't ruling out men forever, but she certainly wasn't about to jump back on the man-wagon with Chuck. She wanted someone quiet and sweet.

Neither word described Chuck Jefferson.

CHUCK WATCHED AS Carly Lewis hurried into her house.

She couldn't get away from him fast enough, and he wasn't

sure why. She'd studied him intently on the way from his mom's to her house. That little smile…he wished he knew what that was all about.

At his house, Chuck couldn't pull in the driveway because Anderson's truck was in the way, so he parked out on the street.

As Chuck got out of his car, Anderson shut off his motor and got out of his truck as well. "So, what the hell was that?"

"Come on in, Andy. It's freezing out here."

Anderson followed him. Chuck's home was right on 38th Street. He considered it a public service that he was sandwiched between college rentals. Knowing a cop lived next door tended to make the kids behave in a bit more civilized manner.

Anderson repeated, "Seriously, what was that? Bringing someone I'd had before me in court to dinner without so much as a warning call."

"Oh, come on. It's not like I brought some hardened criminal." Chuck opened the door, stomped the snow off his feet and hurried in, with Anderson on his heels.

"Still." Anderson took off his coat and tossed it on the stair railing. Chuck threw his coat on top of Anderson's.

The nice thing about being a bachelor was that no one fussed if you didn't hang up your coat.

He led the way into the sparsely furnished living room. Two new recliners, a beat-up couch and a TV. What more did a guy need? He flopped into one of the recliners and said, "Hey, you're the one who set us up, in a work-on-the-Safety-Awareness-Program sort of way."

Anderson took the other recliner and scowled in Chuck's general direction. "Yeah, but I didn't imagine she'd be coming to dinner before your first safety day."

"Mom's on a fix-Chuck-up kick, Andy. I needed camouflage, and Carly fit the bill. Mom was practically swooning." Oh, yeah, his mother would be off his case for a while at least. Maybe he could even talk Carly into coming over another Sunday?

"Yeah, well, after you and Carly left, your mom started on me," Anderson complained. "She told me it had been a year, that I needed to think about dating again. Julia wouldn't want me to be alone."

Chuck didn't know what to say to that. A real guy would just grunt some response, and that was his initial inclination, but he knew that Anderson wasn't the type to open up at all to anyone, so he figured if he didn't say something, no one else would have the opportunity. It looked as if he'd just have to take one for the team.

"Mom and Dad love you," he managed to say, though he felt more than a little emasculated. Still, he forced himself to continue, "At first, it was just that you were Julia's husband, but then it was just for you. We all miss her, but all of us want you to be happy."

Thank goodness none of the guys at the station could hear this conversation. They'd never let him live it down. "Mom and Dad are right, Julia would want you to be happy. And since I'm feeling like some touchy-feely talk show host, let's just forget I said those words."

"Happy to. Because I'm not ready. I don't know if I ever will be ready to move on." As if that was all he could manage in the let's-share-our-emotions department, Anderson changed the subject back to Carly. "So what about you and the pyro?"

"*Accidental arsonist* is her preferred title, if you don't mind." He chuckled at the memory of her using the phrase.

Working with Carly Lewis throughout January was going to be interesting.

Chapter Four

On Monday, Carly hurried home from St. Vincent's. She was working the seven-to-three shift on weekdays for now. Once she passed her boards, she'd be working three twelve-hour shifts a week if she stayed at the hospital.

She'd had to go to the nurse supervisor with her list of Safety Awareness days and request them off. Thankfully, Claire knew about her legal problems and was sympathetic. As a graduate nurse, Carly was under supervision. Claire had juggled the schedule so that Carly could make the program's dates.

After she passed her boards and was a registered nurse, it would be harder to have this kind of flexibility.

Of course, she could go look for another job, straight days, in an office, like Samantha. She'd enjoyed her day at Dr. Jackson's.

Mulling over the pros and cons of both options, she opened her door to chaos. The kids walked home from school and got there about fifteen minutes before she did, but those fifteen minutes gave them time to arm themselves.

"Mom, Mom, Mom," Sean chanted, as she walked into the house and threw her bag by the door.

Carly knew that particular "Mom, Mom, Mom" meant

that Sean was going to ask for something. Something she might not be inclined to grant. She tried to pretend not to notice he wanted something. "Hi, honey, how was your day at school?"

"Fine."

Fine was Sean's standard response.

Sometimes, he actually gave her more than a monosyllabic answer and said, *okay*. Although any description of his day that took more than those one or two syllables was rare, she continued to ask.

"Can we go to Books Galore?" he asked, getting to his Mom-Mom-Mom point. "My new comics should be in and I really need them."

"You don't need them, you want them. And I don't know why you do, comics are dumb," Rhiana proclaimed.

It was an old argument in this house. Sean was an ardent comic fan, and Rhiana used that knowledge to tease him. Having two kids only ten months apart meant teasing was one of their favorite occupations.

"They're not dumb," Sean proclaimed, right on cue. "They're like today's mythology. That new Joss Whedon one…"

As Sean waxed poetic about his friend Jake's theory on comic mythology, Carly tried to escape to her room. All she wanted was five minutes of peace and quiet in order to change out of her scrubs and into her real-people clothes. She didn't even manage to make it out of the kitchen.

"Hey, Mom, can we go, huh?" Sean pressed.

"And if we're taking dork-boy to Books Galore, could we stop at the mall afterward? I wanted to get a new hoody at American Eagle. They're having a sale and I still have that coupon."

Carly did the math in her head and finally nodded. "I have PTA tonight, so here's what we'll do. Give me a few minutes to change, and both of you get ready. We'll stop at Books Galore, then at American Eagle. We can come down Peach Street on the way home and grab something for dinner—"

"Taco Bell," Sean practically screamed.

"McDonald's," Rhiana retorted.

Carly listened as the debate over comics turned into a debate over which fast-food joint's food was preferable.

This time she managed to sneak out without being caught. She hurried down the hall, dodging Sean's boots which sat outside his bedroom—why, she wasn't sure. They should be in the front hall. Next came Rhiana's room. The door was firmly closed with a hand-printed warning—Keep Out—firmly in place. Finally, she got into to her own room and shut the door, then fell on her bed and took a deep breath.

There were days when it all got to be too much. When all she wanted was ten minutes to herself. Even now, she could hear the kids' muted argument, and wished it was quiet.

Which should have made those weekends when Dean had the kids something she looked forward to. Instead, she found those endless hours of silence went from welcomed to oppressive too fast. She longed for a happy medium.

There were thuds on the door. "Mom, can we go through the drive-through at both Taco Bell and McDonalds?" Sean called.

"Yeah, we tried to work out a compromise, like you say we should," Rhiana hollered.

Carly dragged herself up off the bed, knowing her momentary break was over. "Yes, we can," she called answered as she started to change, "if you both agree to come home and start your homework right after dinner with no stalling or complaints. I have a PTA meeting tonight, and I want that done before I go."

"Sure," they called out together.

Carly finished changing, trying to gear herself up for an evening of chaos. If she was lucky, she'd make the meeting on time.

Luck was not on her side.

Despite her best-laid plans, Carly arrived at the PTA meeting at seven-forty-five. She'd have been close to on time, except that at some point between returning from Books Galore and the mall and leaving for the meeting, it had snowed another couple of inches, and she'd had to shovel out the driveway before leaving.

She hurried into the cafeteria and scanned the room for her friends. She spotted Samantha, Michelle and Michelle's new fiancé in a far corner. Samantha saw Carly and gave a little wave. Carly tried to look as inconspicuous as possible as she made her way over to them.

"Where's Harry?" Carly asked quietly as she pulled a chair from a neighboring table over to theirs.

"He's got to do his duty as principal at these things." Samantha pointed to Harry, up at the head table with Heidi, the overworked PTA president who'd roped all three of them onto the Social Planning Committee. There was another guy standing at the microphone.

"Who's the speaker?"

"He's talking about teaching your kids to be fearless," Michelle whispered. "He claims they need to be fearless in order to stand up to peer pressure, less-than-perfect home environments, being in a broken family and all the other outside influences."

Carly nodded, and turned her attention to the speaker.

"…fear can be paralyzing," he was saying, "but that same

fear can push our kids down the wrong path. Bullies for instance are some of the most terrified people there are. They…"

Carly listened to the man as he continued talking about bullies and realized he was describing Dean. Not that Dean had ever physically abused her, but he'd eroded so much of who she was subtly, slowly. And she'd allowed it to happen.

Dean had been there when her parents died, when she so desperately needed something—someone—to cling to. He'd taken over, kept her going during that trying time. And without even knowing it, she'd allowed herself to disappear.

Innocuously, quietly, she'd changed from who she was into who he wanted her—maybe even needed her—to be.

She'd been so afraid of being alone that she hadn't noticed what was really happening to her.

She'd let herself become a doormat, an extension of Dean.

She couldn't blame him. And by the time she'd recognized and admitted it, it was too late.

Samantha gently elbowed her. "Hey, what's that expression all about?"

Michelle was next to Daniel on the other side of the table. They leaned toward each other. Not cuddling, but touching. Barely touching, yet needing that connection.

Something like that was absolutely the last thing Carly ever wanted again. She didn't want to need anyone. She'd needed Dean and lost herself. She couldn't allow that to happen again.

"I'm fine," she assured Samantha, who didn't look convinced. "Really. I'm better than fine. I'm better than I've been in a very long time."

As the other Erie Elementary parents started to clap, she looked up. The speaker had finished. She clapped as well.

Harry stood and went to the mic. "I want to thank everyone

for coming out on such a snowy January night. There are refreshments, thanks to the second-grade parents." He started to move away from the microphone, and perpetually perky Heidi jumped up. "I just want to remind the parents to sign their children's class list. The class with the most parents in attendance tonight will have chips tomorrow."

"Ah, it's all about the reward," Samantha said. "My four make me come because they each want their class to win."

"Sean and Rhiana asked at the beginning of the year if my attendance counted twice for them, since they're both in the same grade. They wanted to go protest to Harry when they found out it didn't."

They walked toward the refreshment line.

"I'll probably stick to a diet soda," Samantha said, even as she eyed the tiny mini cheesecakes longingly.

Harry came up behind her and gave her a discreet hug. "Get the cheesecake. I like a woman with a few curves."

"Any more curves and I'll be the Ravine Flyer," she muttered, naming the new roller coaster at the local amusement park, Waldemeer.

Harry leaned down and quickly, before anyone noticed, kissed the nape of her neck. "You're perfect just the way you are. Every curve—" He leaned closer and whispered the rest of his compliment.

Whatever he said had Samantha blushing profusely.

Carly felt a warmth spread through her middle…it was almost a longing. A tiny little niggle of a thought that some day, she might want that. What Samantha and Harry had.

She brutally pushed the thought back. What Samantha and Harry had was unique. Special. That didn't mean everyone was destined for something like that.

Of course, Michelle had found Daniel. She looked at them,

farther down the line. They weren't as openly affectionate as Samantha and Harry, but when Michelle reached out and grabbed a napkin for Daniel, their hands brushed. And they paused. It was only a split second. Carly was pretty sure no one else noticed, but she did. And that pang hit again.

She sighed.

"Something wrong?" Samantha asked, as Harry turned around to talk to one of the parents.

Carly shook her head and reached for a chocolate cupcake. "Nothing at all. Simply looking for a chocolate fix."

"Hey, the one thing PTA moms have down to a science is chocolate. I don't think I've ever been to one of these when I didn't find myself rewarded by something chocolate afterward. Even when I was actively dieting, PTA nights didn't count. Or at least they didn't count much."

Before Carly could echo Harry's reassurances that Samantha was perfect just the way she was, Samantha said, "Thankfully, I don't worry about dieting much anymore— well, at least I don't worry very much."

Carly smiled. "Harry's good for you."

"Yeah. It sounds totally lame, but he gets me, and likes me anyway."

"Who likes you?" Harry said, rejoining their conversation.

"You like me."

"You got that." He walked with them toward the table, then groaned. "I think I have to put my principal hat back on." He gestured at a mom Carly didn't know, who was waving wildly in their direction. He reached out, took Samantha's hand and gave it a quick squeeze. "Be back in a minute."

Samantha's eyes locked on him as he made his way over to the other table.

Carly studied Samantha watching Harry.

She wondered if she'd ever gotten that goofy look on her face watching Dean. She tried to remember when they were first together. Tried to remember a time when she'd loved him so much that she couldn't keep her eyes off him—and she couldn't.

Had she merely forgotten?

Or had she and Dean never had the kind of connection Samantha and Harry had?

Or Michelle and Daniel.

She glanced across the table to see Michelle smiling at something Daniel had said to her.

Carly tried to assure herself that she didn't want what they had. That she was fine. She was a strong, self-sufficient woman who enjoyed standing on her own two feet.

That much was true. But somehow it sounded sort of lonely.

AT ONE-THIRTY THE next afternoon, Chuck reveled in the fact that the presentation of the first Safety Awareness Program appeared to be a success.

He should be resting on his laurels, but right then, the only thing resting was his gaze on Carly Lewis. She was sitting across from him in the gym talking to another group of students, handing out pamphlets as she smiled and laughed.

Animated.

That was the word he'd use to describe her.

Well, that was the word except when she had been in his company today.

Monosyllabic was closer to the mark then.

She was still obviously annoyed about dinner.

They'd been in this gym all morning and, rather than feeling punished, Carly seemed to be having a grand time with everyone. Including Bob, an Erie firefighter who was sitting next to her.

Chuck knew Bob from working with him on creating the program. He knew the guy was young and single. But despite being single, he rarely lacked for female companionship, according to rumors. Widely varied female companionship.

And from what Chuck knew about Carly's break-up, the last guy in the world that she should consider dating was a womanizer.

He smiled at his use of the word. He sounded like his mom. Thankfully he'd only thought of the word and not said it out loud.

"So, sir, if I want to be a police officer when I get older, what do I need to do?" a skinny kid asked.

Chuck had been answering the same question most of the day. By rote he started the spiel, then noticed Carly was in between groups of kids and was laughing at something Bob said.

Chuck tried to ignore them as he put together a stack of his handouts and gave them to the kid. "There's information on law enforcement in there, but there's also info you need now about Internet safety, dealing with bullies and the like."

The kid took the stack and moved on to the paramedics. Chuck tried not to think about the fact the paramedics had brought all kinds of cool equipment that enthralled the kids. Oh, he'd brought along some handcuffs and patches, but it wasn't quite the same as a stethoscope or gurney.

The principal came over to him. "I think that's it, Lieutenant. We'd like to thank you for bringing all your people today. The kids had a great time."

Chuck made small talk while he started cleaning up his pamphlets until the principal moved on down the line, then he glanced across the gym to see Carly picking up her material as well, placing it neatly into a plastic crate she'd brought along.

He hurried to finish, wanting to catch her before she escaped. He got over just as she slipped her coat on. "See, that wasn't so bad, was it?"

"No, Lieutenant." She paused a pregnant moment and added, "Lieutenant, sir."

"Come on, Carly, I said I was sorry I didn't tell you about Julia." He felt ten years old, but resisted the urge to ball his hands into fists and shove them in his pockets, or shuffle his feet back and forth. He managed to hold himself steady, but still, mentally, his fists were in his pockets.

Carly didn't say anything, then surprised him by asking, "You could do something for me, though."

"What? Just name it." A reprieve. Maybe she wasn't as annoyed as he thought.

She reached into her bag and pulled out an envelope that from all appearances had a card in it. "Give this to your brother-in-law."

He took the thick envelope and their hands touched. He enjoyed it. "What is it?"

"An apology."

"Carly, you were exactly what Anderson needed. Someone who would challenge him—who wasn't awed by the fact he was a judge. He liked sparring with you." His voice softened, just as it always did when he spoke about Julia. "We all miss my sister, but it's been a year. Anderson needs to start healing and moving on."

"And moving on is easier said than done for some people."

"Easy or not—" Chuck was going to say that easy or not, Anderson had to figure out a way to get on with his life, but he realized they weren't only talking about his brother-in-law.

Carly had been hurt by her ex. Chuck didn't have to be overly astute to know that. If nothing else, burning down half her neighborhood served as a clear sign.

So rather than finishing the sentence, he said, "Listen, our next gig is on Friday. What if afterward you and I go out?"

"Out?" There was confusion in her voice, which didn't surprise Chuck since he was rather confused as well. He hadn't meant to ask her on a date, but it appeared that's what he'd done.

In for a penny, in for a pound, he figured, and continued, "Yes, out. For a drink—"

"It will only be two in the afternoon." She set down the plastic bin she'd been holding. "I don't drink at two."

"It's closer to two-thirty by the time we pack up." He grinned.

"And I have kids who are coming at two-thirty."

"Fine. We could pick them up and all go out to—" he tried to think of an appropriate place, and settled on "—Chuck E. Cheese or some other kid-friendly spot."

"They're in seventh grade. Chuck E. Cheese is a bit too young. And anyway, my ex is picking them up from school on Friday. They're going to Cleveland and spending the weekend at his mom's. It's her birthday."

"So why did you mention kids?"

Carly had an expression as if she'd been busted, as she answered, "I thought it would be an easy way to turn down going for coffee with you."

"I meant what I said about Andy moving on, and the same applies to you. And what better way to start than by going out with one of Erie's finest?"

"So, this isn't coffee…it's a date?" When he didn't immediately answer Carly added, "I want things clear in my head because the idea of us dating immediately muddied everything."

He wasn't sure he'd originally meant it as a date, but suddenly, he very much wanted it to be.

Out of the corner of his eye he saw Bob, the firefighter, making his way toward them, so he picked up Carly's crate and put it on top of his own. "Come on, I'll walk you to your car."

As they walked away from Bob toward the exit, he said, "And I'm going to make a stab in the dark that you haven't dated anyone since your ex, right?"

She nodded and asked, "Why?"

"Well, if you're going to move on, I'm the perfect guy because I don't ever date any woman more than six weeks."

"Pardon? You put a time limit on your dating?"

They walked out of the gym and were hit by a frigid blast of air. "You should zip up your coat," Chuck said before he could stop himself.

"I'm fine," Carly huffed. Even if he hadn't heard the verbal huff on indication, he couldn't help notice the huge puff of warm air turn to vapor in the cold.

"And you're avoiding my question," she continued, coat still unzipped. "You have a dating time limit?"

He decided to ignore the fact her coat was still flapping in the wind and answered. "It's not something I sat down and analyzed, but it is the way it always works out. After a month or so, women begin to get possessive, and frankly, I'm not interested in long-term relationshiops."

Chuck had many reasons—rationalizations—for avoiding longer relationships. A cop's schedule was crazy. On four days, off two. Shift changes monthly. Granted Chuck's new job was a same-shift, weekdays sort of one, but it didn't alter the fact that statistically, relationships didn't go so well for cops.

"So, I should go out with you because it won't last more than a few weeks?" Carly asked as they reached her van. She popped the back end, took her crate from him and stowed it inside, then turned, watching him as she waited for his response.

"I'm the perfect practice date. You'll be seeing me at the rest of our program afternoons anyway. We'll just go out a few times after, or in between. Then when they're over, we'll both move on."

She cocked her head to one side, and studied him, then asked, "Why on earth would you want to date me? A pyro-maniac mother of two?"

Now, that was a question that Chuck wasn't going to dwell on. So, he simply corrected her. "Accidental arsonist, not pyro."

She smiled. The expression looked good on her. "You're serious about a date on Friday?"

"Yes."

She nodded. "Okay, I guess after five hours in a gym with kids, a coffee might be nice."

"Hey, I'll even spring for something to go with it."

"Donuts?" she teased and walked toward the front of the van and the driver's-side door.

He groaned. "Even if I was a huge donut fan, I'd boycott them simply so I didn't feed into that old cop-eating-donuts stereotype. I was thinking pie."

She laughed then. It wasn't some dainty sort of sound, or even a girlish giggle. It was a full-throated sound that Chuck knew he'd like to hear more of.

"Fine. I don't think you really know what you're doing, but yes, we'll go out after the program on Friday."

Chuck didn't tell her that that made two of them who didn't know what he was doing. He simply smiled. "Friday then."

She unlocked her door and climbed into the seat. And it

was a bit of a climb. The fact she was so tiny was really accentuated as she sat in the giant vehicle.

"Thanks," she said. "I'd better run or I'll be late picking up the kids. I'll see you Friday."

"See you then."

He stood in the parking lot, holding his box and watched her pull away.

What on earth had he just done?

"Hey, nice job—" Bob said.

Chuck turned around. "Thanks for participating. It seemed to go well."

"Just wanted to say I wasn't trying to poach." He nodded at Carly's van as it pulled out of the school's parking lot and onto the street. "I didn't know she was spoken for."

"Huh?" Chuck managed. Spoken for? He didn't really think of his going out with Carly as her being "spoken for."

"You and Carly. She's nice, but I don't date other men's women."

Before Chuck could respond that coffee and pie didn't make Carly taken, Bob continued, "I don't need to. There are plenty of available ones out there for the taking."

Chuck didn't even begin to know what to say to that, so he mumbled a quick thank you and hurried to his car. The unmarked Crown Vic was a perk of the new position. He put his box of information in the trunk; the card that Carly had given him for Anderson was on top. Rather than go straight to the station, he'd stop by Anderson's office. He didn't want to upset Carly on Friday by not having delivered her card.

Fifteen minutes later, he parked his car at the police station, and walked the block to the County Courthouse with its two-story columns lining the front. Chuck didn't know anything about architecture, but the Courthouse always made him think of Greek plays.

The sidewalks were pretty well shoveled, so it wasn't a bad walk, but it was a cold one. Unlike Carly, he zipped his coat against the freezing air that blew in off the lake. But despite that precaution the warmth of the courthouse hit him as he waited in line to be cleared by security before going about halfway down the east wing to the stairs to the second floor. Andy's door was closed, which boded well.

"He in?" he asked Joyce.

She nodded. "Go on back."

Andy's office was everything a person who grew up watching television lawyer shows would expect. Built-in shelves with a dark mahogany-colored stain lined with beautifully bound legal books. The walls were a light tan, the fact that they were nondescript made them simply accentuate the Civil War paintings Anderson had on every available wall space.

Chuck knew that they were by Dale Gallon, a Gettysburg artist Anderson was passionate about collecting.

Chuck put the envelope on the desk in front of Anderson. "This is for you."

His brother-in-law picked up the envelope, holding it gingerly as if he expected it to blow up or something. "What is it?"

"It's from Carly."

Looking even more wary, Anderson opened it.

Chuck had been right. It was a card. But not something she'd run down to the card store to buy.

"Did she make this?" Anderson held the card out toward Chuck to give him a better view of it.

Chuck took it. "I have no idea."

The paper was thick and sort of tannish-colored. It wasn't smooth, but had a slightly uneven texture. It took a moment for Chuck to realize it looked more like material than paper. There was a fern on the front. Not some drawn-on thing, but a dried real fern that was sort of glued in place.

Chuck handed it over. "Yeah, it's homemade."

"Carly doesn't strike me as someone who does crafts. Still…" Anderson examined it, as if weighing it. "Beautifully made by hand. Julia would have gone crazy over cards like this."

"Maybe Carly bought it. What's it say?"

Anderson shook his head, then read, "'Dear Andy,'" a smile played lightly on his lips as he read her greeting. "'I just want to apologize for picking on you at dinner. Especially after you explained why you sentenced me to a month working with your brother-in-law. Although a month working with Chuck could be construed as cruel and unusual punishment, it's obvious your heart was in the right place. Thank you. Finding a job will be easier without an arson record. Warmly, Carly Lewis.'"

Anderson held the now-opened card out for Chuck to see. "Look, she did it in calligraphy, by hand. There's no way she bought it."

Chuck looked at the letter. "Yeah, she must have made this."

The idea of Carly taking the time to do something like this struck him as incongruent. "The part about working with me was a dig. She was pissed that I let her verbally spar with you at dinner without telling her about Julia."

Anderson's smile faded. "Why?"

"I guess because she figured picking on a guy who's still mourning after a year was rather like kicking a dog when it was down."

"You're going to put a time limit on mourning, too?" He frowned.

"Mom's right, Anderson. Don't tell her I said those words." Chuck meant that as a joke, but Anderson wasn't biting. "It's time for you to move on. Carly, too. She's got to get over her bitterness about her ex, and you…"

"Me?"

Feeling nauseatingly touchy-feely, Chuck took a deep breath then blurted out, "You can't hang on to the past. Julia wouldn't want that for you. Carly's taken her first steps, now it's time for you to, too."

"What do you mean, Carly taking steps?"

"Despite some initial reluctance, it seems she's jumping into the dating pool again." Chuck tried not to look smug, but it was hard.

Anderson's grin was back. "Anyone I know?"

"Yeah. You could say that."

Anderson nodded. "You're sure about this?"

"Hey, I told her—I'm the perfect practice date for her. Just a rebound guy. Nothing serious. No expectations of forever. I was clear about that, Andy. I wouldn't lead any woman on, especially Carly Lewis." He wasn't sure why especially Carly, but there it was. He wouldn't be able to stand hurting her.

"It sounds good when you put it that way, but be careful, Chuck."

"Why?"

"Carly doesn't strike me as a woman who's simple to date." Anderson laughed as he held up the handcrafted card. "I suspect there's a lot to Carly Lewis that none of us suspect."

Chuck didn't say anything, but silently he agreed.

There was a lot more to Carly Lewis than he'd initially thought…and he couldn't wait to find out more.

Chapter Five

Friday morning, Rhiana screamed in frustration. The sound was loud enough that Rhiana's voice carried from her room down the hall to Carly's where she was desperately trying to decide what would be the appropriate outfit to wear at a Safety Awareness Program that would also be suitable for a date.

"Mom, I can't stay over at Dad's without my red pajama pants. Where'd you put them?"

"I didn't put them anywhere, Rhi."

A date. It had been more than a decade since Carly had dated. She'd been all full of suggestions when Samantha had had dating angst and when Michelle had gotten confused over her relationship with Daniel. But now, here she was getting ready for her own date, and she didn't have any suggestions for herself.

She finally gave up and dove into the stack of clothes she'd made on her bed, grabbing a pair of dressy denim trousers and a white turtleneck sweater. Even though the pants were dressier than regular jeans, they were still denim. And she wore sweaters on a daily basis in the winter, so it wasn't anything extraordinary. She didn't want Chuck to think she'd fussed over her clothes.

And she also didn't want him to think she hadn't given them a thought.

Jeans and a sweater conveyed both messages, she decided.

"Come on, Mom," Rhiana called again. "They went into the laundry on Monday. You still haven't done them?"

Carly stopped picking up the excess clothing on her bed and hung the items back up before storming to Rhiana's room.

As she'd expected, the floor was littered with a week's worth of dirty clothes, notebooks, wadded-up papers and probably half the dishes in the house. Carly scanned the mess and spied the pajama pants in the corner, one leg sticking out from behind the chair that Rhiana used as her version of a dirty clothes hamper.

Carly didn't say anything, just pointed.

Rhiana turned around and spotted the pajama leg. "Oh, great. They're dirty. Now I've got nothing to wear at Dad's this weekend."

"You have more than one pair of pajama pants."

"Yes, but you didn't wash any of them. The only things of mine on the table in the laundry room were two sweatshirts, a pair of jeans and a few pairs of socks." She dropped her voice. "I don't even have any clean underwear for next week. I guess you should do another load of laundry, huh?"

There were times Carly almost exploded with pride in her kids, but there were a growing number of times when pride was the exact opposite of what she was feeling.

This was one of those opposite-of-pride times.

She counted to ten before answering. "I guess you'd better go get a garbage bag, shove all your clothes in it and take it to your father's with you. His condo has a washer and dryer, right?"

"Mom, they stack one on top of the other. It would take me five or six loads to get all this washed. It would take a whole day."

She forced a smile. "Lucky for you, there's both Saturday and Sunday left to get it all done. Otherwise, next week might be difficult with no clean underwear."

"Mooommm."

"Rhiana, you officially just took on doing all your own laundry. I've shown you how the machine works, how to do it. Now, it's yours. You're responsible for getting done what needs done."

"But Mom…"

"Maybe after a few weeks of attending to your own laundry, you'll be a bit more considerate. I've had a crazy busy week. I got up at five in order to get things done around the house, including the laundry, so that I'd have everything ready for you two when you went to your dad's today after school."

"But you didn't do all my clothes," Rhiana whined.

"I told you that I'd be doing the laundry and assumed you'd brought me everything you wanted done." Thinking that settled that, Carly left Rhiana's room.

"But Mom," Rhiana repeated as she followed Carly into the hall, "you used to come in and pick my clothes up for me."

"And that was my mistake. I'm sorry for that. It's time you found out that things aren't the same."

"Right. You're always too busy to give me what I need now."

Part of Carly wanted to scream, *what about what I need?* Another part of her wanted to cringe. She'd worked so hard trying to keep it all together and to be sure the kids' needs were met. Having Rhiana say she hadn't managed hurt.

But she knew her daughter was also hurting, so rather than lashing out, Carly simply hugged her. "I am busy. But even if I wasn't working, I hope I'd have figured out that babying you wasn't doing you any favors. You have to learn to stand on your own two feet."

"Great mom you are. You break up our family, burn down the neighborhood and then abandon your kids. Nice going, Mom." Rhiana turned around, stomped to her room and slammed the door behind her.

Rhiana's words hit dead-on.

Nice going, Carly.

Maybe her fight with Rhiana set the mood for the day's Safety Awareness Program. It seemed none of the kids would meet her eye. She smiled, she handed out pamphlets, yet rather than talking with her and asking questions, they acted as if she was infected with some kind of mysterious plague.

It was the longest five hours of her life.

Afterward, Chuck had followed her home, where she'd dropped off her car, and got in his. Now, she was sitting in the car next to Chuck, feeling more and more uncomfortable and out of place.

She longed to turn to him and say, "take me home." She didn't know what to do, what to say. And feeling this out of place and awkward only added to her already sour mood.

"Carly, are you okay?"

"No," she admitted. "It's been a lousy sort of day. Rhiana and I had a fight, the kids at that school were not nearly as…"

"Friendly?" he finished for her. "Listen, it wasn't just you. They didn't have much to say to me either. When I tried to give them information on law enforcement, they gave me a look like being a cop was the last thing they'd ever do, and when I handed out safety info, a few actually scoffed. It was a tough crowd. That sometimes happens. It's over now though. Your day's looking up."

"No, it's not." She wished she could suck the words in again because she knew she sounded as petulant as Rhiana had.

'Hey, I think I resent that."

"Don't resent it. It's not you, it's me."

Chuck glanced at her and shook his head. "That phrase is the kiss of death. All men fear it."

She turned away from Chuck, not wanting to see his expression. It was easier to watch at the snow-covered houses out the window. "But it is me. I don't know what to do about anything," she admitted. "Rhiana is entering that difficult age for girls. My mom always said girls were easy until they hit their teens, and she hoped that in my twenties I'd like her again. It didn't take me nearly that long. I'm hoping the same's true for Rhiana. And it's not just the kids. This. I don't know how to date. Even something as casual as this is supposed to be."

There. She'd said the words. Admitted how very lame she was. She glanced away from the window and stole a peek at Chuck.

He didn't seem concerned by her revelation. He simply shrugged. "Take a deep breath, Carly. It's not really our first. It's our second if you count dinner at my parents."

"I don't. You invited me there as a front to keep your mother off your back. That's not a date. That's subterfuge."

He laughed. "Fair enough, then. So let me help you out, this is the point where I tell you that although I know I said it'd be coffee, since your kids are gone, I thought I'd bump it up a bit. We're going to Joe Roots for a late lunch, early dinner. Then, maybe a drive around the peninsula. I love it down there this time of year. It's not really warm enough to walk, but it's beautiful to look at the ice dunes. I know a place where we can park and see them. And on the drive, and afterward, we'll converse and get to know each other better. It's not hard."

"You already know more about me than you probably should. My divorce, the arson—"

"Accidental arson," he corrected, then glanced over at her with a huge grin on his face.

She laughed despite her nerves. "Yes. Accidental arson sounds so much nicer. But there's more. You've already seen me crying, embarrassed and more than a little snarky."

He shrugged again. "And I still asked you out. So relax. I've seen you at your worst moments, so what else can happen? Now, tell me about your day."

"Not much to tell. Well, other than the fact that I had a fight with my daughter this morning. She seems to be of the opinion that I've ruined her life. I'm not sure it's not true."

"How old is she?"

"Eleven, almost twelve. Almost a teen." At twelve, Sean was only one birthday away from being a teen. It seemed like yesterday they were both babies. They'd both loved and adored her. She could remember the feel of them, pressed against her as she rocked them. That baby scent. The magic of their smiles.

Rhiana wasn't smiling now.

"Most kids that age are convinced of that. It will get worse for a few years, but eventually they'll move away from home and come to understand how wonderful you were," Chuck assured her.

Carly recalled that's just what had happened when she went away to college. Suddenly her mother, who throughout her teens had felt like a warden, became her best friend. She wished she'd have known how short their time together would be. She'd have done more, called more.

She was pretty sure those sad thoughts hadn't been Chuck's intent, so she turned the tables. "Your turn. How was your day?"

"Same old, same old. Went into work early, met with the reporter from the paper, filled out a few forms, then came to the Safety Awareness Program. My job isn't very *NYPD Blue*. As you've pointed out, I do know a bit more about you than you know about me, so ask me something."

There was one question that had been begging to be asked. The old Carly—the don't rock the boat Carly—probably would have let it go, but the new Carly went ahead and asked, "Why do you only date short-term?"

Rather than look offended, Chuck glanced away from the road to her and smiled. "That's easy. Being a cop is tough. Swing shifts, working holidays. It's hard on us, although it's harder on families and significant others. I've seen a lot of guys end up divorced, and I don't want to go that route. If I ever married, I'd want what my parents have, and I don't see many cops with that kind of relationship, so I'll just forgo for something less. I always make sure the women I'm dating understand there's no forever for us. A few weeks of good companionship, and then we both go our own ways. No re-criminations. No looking back. It's neater. Easier."

Carly thought through his explanation. It made sense. And on some level, she really could identify with what he was saying. Nothing in her wanted a serious relationship again. Yet…

She finally said, "Oh."

Chuck pulled to a stop at a light on 12th Street, and this time turned her way and didn't just glance. He really looked at her, as if he really saw her. That was something she wasn't sure Dean had ever done—really seen her.

"Carly, I know we're rather new acquaintances, but I recognize that your 'oh' means you don't agree. It's not like you to hold anything back."

"It's not for me to agree or disagree," she said primly.

A car behind them honked, and Chuck began driving. "Come on, you can tell me. Spit it out."

"Well," she replied slowly, weighing her words. "It seems to me that's a cop-out, pardon my pun."

"How so?"

"You worry about divorce, so you never allow a relationship to progress beyond the superficial? Sounds like you're scared, so you've set up a comfortable dating criteria that protects you."

Chuck was busy navigating the busy 12th Street traffic, which meant she was able to study him at will. And she could tell by his expression—the way his brow bunched up and he frowned—that he didn't like her analysis.

"Not that it's any of my business," she added quickly. "I'm scared, too, and I doubt I'll ever do more than superficial dating again."

His frown evaporated as he exclaimed, "Wow, we're two of the most upbeat people around."

"Hmm-mmm. Is this how most of your dates go?" she teased. "If so, I'm pretty sure that my plan to avoid too much of this kind of thing is a good one."

"No, Carly, I'd have to say everything about you—from the way that we met, to our first date—is unique."

And despite his smile, Carly wasn't the least bit sure that was a compliment.

SOMEHOW THEY MADE THEIR way through a late lunch at Joe Roots, but it was close. Chuck didn't think of himself as someone afraid of commitment, he thought of himself as a pragmatist. An upbeat pragmatic person.

After they'd eaten, they drove around Presque Isle. He found a perfect parking space beyond one of the far beaches where they could sit in the car, and see the ice dunes, which had been formed when the lake turned to ice and the waves and spray froze.

"I don't think I've ever come down here in the winter," Carly said. "But I wish I had. It's beautiful. It's as if a wave was coming in off the lake, and just froze."

She leaned forward to get a better look. "Can we go out?"

She'd only worn a coat to the program. No hat, no gloves, no scarf. Rather than point that out, he simply said, "It's only in the twenties."

"That's fine. I'm game if you are."

"Hang on a minute." He reached behind his seat and pulled out his work bag and dug around. "Here, put these on."

She took the hat and the thick gloves he handed her. "I don't need to—"

"Like you said, you don't come down here this time of year."

"But what about you?"

He reached into his coat pocket and pulled out his own hat and gloves. "I'm good. And I know you'd never let your kids out in this weather without a hat. Just wear them, okay? Please?"

For a moment, he thought she was going to argue. It seemed that Carly felt compelled to resist doing what she was told. Asking seemed to work better because she nodded.

"Yes, Mom," she teased. Dressed, she opened the door and stepped outside.

He followed and didn't mention his gloves looked absurdly large on her hands. Really absurdly large.

"We can't stay long. It'll be getting dark and the park closes soon."

"I just want to go out on the dunes for a minute."

He grabbed her arm before she could dart off toward them.

"You can't walk on them. Ice dunes are notoriously fragile, and these are early this year, so they're probably even more so. We can take a short walk along the beach and look at them."

"Now I see why you're a cop. You're bossy."

He couldn't tell if she was teasing, but suspected she wasn't. "I just didn't want to have to jump in and rescue you."

"Don't worry, I've found being rescued doesn't sit well with me," she replied, then started walking far faster than someone as tiny as she was should be able to.

"Carly, wait up. I didn't mean—"

"I know. It's not you, it's me, remember? Let's forget my snit and enjoy the view."

He wasn't sure what had happened. Normally, he'd let it go, but he wanted to figure out Carly Lewis. "Carly?"

"My ex used to think I needed to be rescued, needed his guidance. And for a long time, I was okay with that. But when he left, I discovered the only one I could count on was myself. I don't want to rely on someone else, and I certainly don't want to be rescued by someone else."

"Even if you were drowning?" he joked.

She hesitated, then with a grin and a mock sigh said, "Okay, so if I'm drowning, you can help me. I'm talking literally drowning. Going under, can't breathe. But if I'm figuratively drowning, let me go. Let me figure it out on my own and I'll rescue myself."

He stood next to her and put an arm around her shoulder. "Deal."

They stood and just looked out at the frozen lake for a long time. "We probably should get going before one of the park rangers comes by to kick us out."

"Yeah. But thanks for bringing me here. You live somewhere your whole life and take things for granted. I usually come here in the summer, but never really stopped to think how beautiful it might be in the winter."

He still had his arm around her as they walked back to his car. He was pretty sure Carly hadn't really noticed, otherwise she'd shrug it off and assure him she didn't need anyone to hold her.

Bristles. That's what she wanted everyone to see. But he'd had a glimpse of a woman who found an ice dune beautiful and didn't want to take anything for granted. She had a hard shell with a gooey center.

And he was smart enough not to mention the insight to her.

They seemed to have turned a corner. The ride back across Erie to the east side of town was much more comfortable.

"Well, thanks," she said as he pulled into the drive. "I had a great evening."

"I'll see you to the door." He'd already opened his door, positive Carly wasn't going to sit and wait for him to come around to her side and get her door for her.

He was right.

Carly was out and on her way onto the porch before he caught up. She fumbled in her purse for her keys, then turned to him. For the first time since the ice dune, she looked nervous again. "Well, thanks so much, Chuck."

What now? He tried to jolly her out of whatever had set off this newest onslaught of nerves. "You don't have to sound so happy to have the evening end. Remember, my ego and all that."

"I'm pretty sure your ego can handle my relief that my official FDSD—"

"FDSD?" he asked.

"First date since divorce. Anyway, I think your ego can handle that I'm relieved it's over. It was another hurdle I had to overcome."

"A hurdle? You know, a guy could get real conceited with all the compliments you bandy around." There was an edge to his comment, he heard it and wondered if Carly noticed. She didn't give any indication. Didn't seem contrite or embarrassed.

Bristles, he reminded himself. He just needed to get underneath the bristles. "And if we counted that meal at my mom's, it's a second date. And they both went really well."

"Your mom's did not go well. You set me up to attack your poor, defenseless, mourning brother-in-law."

"Time out." He made the motion from basketball. Hand over fingertips. "We're not going to discuss Andy."

"No, we're not. It's way too cold to discuss anything out here. I'll talk to you again next week at the Safety Awareness Program."

She put the key in the lock and twisted it, then withdrew it and opened the door. "Again, thanks."

"Wait. I know it's been a while since you dated, but you're forgetting the most important part." And before she started analyzing and debating it, he leaned down and kissed her.

He expected a short, goodnight buss on the lips.

It couldn't be much after six, so all he expected was a good-afternoon kiss. That's all he'd intended. Quickly, the kiss escalated from peck to passion.

At first, he suspected Carly wrapped her arms around his neck as a way of steadying herself, as she stood on tiptoe to allow the kiss to deepen.

Moment by moment, they tasted and explored each other.

Then Carly stepped backward through the open door without breaking contact, and Chuck willingly followed, kicking the door closed behind them.

And still they kissed.

She dropped her purse to the floor with a thud, and Chuck reached behind him to lock the deadbolt.

Carly started to kick off her boots and started wiggling out of her coat, then broke their kiss long enough to say, "You, too."

Part of him—the part that liked to think of himself as a nice guy—thought he should call a halt. As Carly kept pointing out, it had been a long time since she'd dated.

The other part of himself won out and he obliged her, slipping off his leather jacket and tossing it on the floor.

"My room?" she asked.

That stopped him and the nice-guy-part kicked into over-drive. "Carly, are you sure?"

"No, and I don't want to think about it. I don't want to discuss it. I want you. Now. Naked."

That was clear. At her words a mental image of both of them naked flashed through Chuck's mind and all he wanted to do was forget any nice-guy worries. Still, he found himself saying, "I don't want you to wake up regretting—"

"You're afraid of commitment, remember? That makes you perfect. You're used to having unemotional sex. No strings to get tangled up in. I want you," she repeated.

He knew he should walk away because he knew that Carly Lewis was not a sex-on-the-first-date sort of woman.

She wasn't a casual-sex kind of woman.

She was the type of woman you took home to meet your mother.

Yet he wanted her despite his reservations.

She took his hand. "Don't make me beg, Chuck."

"Carly, I'm trying to be a nice guy."

"I don't want a nice guy tonight…I want you." She laughed at her own joke, then tugged him toward the stairs. "One night, Chuck. No commitment. No ever-afters. Just you and me."

"Carly—"

She dropped his hand. "Unless you don't want me." The openness, the teasing evaporated, and in their place, Carly's wariness returned. Maybe it was more than that. Maybe it was resignation. As if being rejected was what she expected.

That look on her face tore at him. Needing to dispel that concern immediately, Chuck swept her into his arms—she weighed next to nothing—and carried her up the stairs. "Do I want you? I'm about to explode with wanting you."

"Oh, man, I feel like Scarlett O'Hara."

"Frankly, my dear…" He kissed her again as he topped the stairs. "Which way?"

"Straight."

He carried her into the bedroom. He wasn't sure what he'd expected. Something serviceable, utilitarian. But what he found was greens, bright yellows and pinks. Lace and flowers.

A room that looked completely and decidedly feminine.

"You can set me down now, Chuck."

"This room isn't what I expected."

Carly sighed. "What is it about me that makes everyone so surprised that I like girly, lacy things, or that I enjoy doing crafts? See that afghan on the bottom of the bed?"

There was a white afghan with yellow and pink flowers accented by green leaves that sort of stuck up all over it. "Yeah."

"I made that. And the throw pillows, and the curtains. I enjoy that kind of stuff." Carly's bristles were back in place.

Chuck immediately tried to undo whatever his unthinking comment had done. "I didn't mean to insult you."

"You didn't. I'm used to it. I didn't mean to throw a damper on things by getting defensive."

"Carly, I don't think you could throw a damper on anything." So, saying, he leaned down and kissed her again, his hands moving toward her waist then upwards, cupping her breasts. "I want—"

The doorbell rang, and even from all the way up in the bedroom, they could hear loud, hurried thumps against the door as well, as the bell convulsively kept ringing. "Can we ignore it?"

"Probably not." She kissed him firmly, then straightened her clothes. "Hopefully, I'll only be a minute." She hurried from the room.

Chuck stood in the middle of the uber-feminine bedroom. He thought he had Carly Lewis pegged as an impulsive, passionate woman. And he was sure he was right. Although here in this room, remembering her handmade card for Anderson, he had a growing sense that there was more to her. Much more.

CARLY PICKED UP HER coat and Chuck's and put them on hooks before she opened the door to find Dean and her kids. "Uh, I thought you were keeping the kids this weekend?"

"I was. But I have an important last-minute meeting out-of-town."

Rhiana scowled as Dean offered up his excuse. "Ha. Don't listen to him, Mom. His *meeting* is with *her.*"

Carly didn't have to ask who *her* was. "Gayle?"

Rhiana nodded. "She gave him a surprise weekend at some dumb grown-up love nest, and he'd rather be with her than us and take us to Cleveland for Grandma's birthday. That's fine, 'cause we don't want to be with him either."

"That's enough, Rhi." Carly looked at Sean who hadn't said anything. "You okay?"

He nodded.

Carly thought about sending them to their rooms, but she knew that Chuck was still upstairs. "Fine. Both of you head into the living room. I'll be right in."

She turned to her ex. His expression while Rhiana ranted gave her all the information she needed. "Really, Dean? You're blowing off your mom's birthday?"

"She didn't even know we were coming, so she won't miss us. I sent her flowers."

Carly wished she was surprised, but she wasn't. She'd always felt bad that Dean treated his mother so casually. Not that Darlene Lewis had liked Carly, she'd never known why. But still, she felt bad. She'd have to be sure the kids called tomorrow. Speaking of calling…

"You should have called, Dean. What if I had plans and wasn't here?"

He snorted. "Come on Carly…" His sentence trailed off as he looked at some point behind her.

Carly turned and saw Chuck coming down the stairs.

"Thanks for letting me use the bathroom." Chuck walked up next to Carly then put his left arm around her and extended his right hand to Dean. "Hi, I'm Chuck, and you must be Dean."

Dean didn't take Chuck's extended hand. Instead he turned to Carly. "Who's he?"

"A friend—not that it's any of your business."

"Oh, come on, honey." The endearment rolled off Chuck's tongue as if he'd used it a thousand times. "Good old Dean here is ditching his weekend with the kids in order to go have a tryst with his girlfriend. I'm sure he can handle the idea of your being in a new relationship."

Dean's eyes narrowed as he studied Chuck. His frown said he didn't like what he saw. "How long has this been going on?"

Carly shot a warning look at Chuck, who seemed totally unrepentant, then turned to Dean. "I met Chuck the day I burned the couch. Maybe it was fate. I'd put my past and my bitterness to rest and there he was. Perfect timing."

"I was the first cop on the scene. I'm sure you don't remember. I mean, I saw you there, slinking to the fringes of the crowd, looking embarrassed to be there, but not quite sure you could leave."

"You're a cop?"

"Yes. And both Carly and I would appreciate it if you gave her a little more warning if you're not going to live up to your visitation agreement. We'd been out. If you'd come any earlier, no one would have been home."

"Oh, sure. I'll do that. I'd better be going now." Dean took a few steps toward the living room. "'Bye kids. See you next week." He stepped out onto the porch. "Thanks, Carly."

"Don't thank me, Dean. I can't believe you're going to squander your weekend with the kids, that you're going to pick your girlfriend over your own mother. But then, you never did really appreciate the idea of family." She shut the door on him and turned to Chuck. "Thanks. You shocked him, *honey.*"

"I know you were married to him, but pardon me if I say that man's an ass."

"I couldn't agree more." She felt a bit lighter, knowing that Chuck was on her side. Almost immediately, though, her heart broke as she thought about the kids. It was one thing for Dean to hurt her and quite another for him to cause the kids pain. "Listen, I'd better get in there and see about soothing them."

"I'll leave you to it. Can I see you again this week?" he asked as he put on his coat.

She nodded. "Let's talk the logistics at the next program presentation."

"Great. See you Tuesday." He glanced around and leaned down and kissed her.

It was a short kiss, but it left Carly feeling all weak-in-the-knees and girlishly breathless again. It made her want to forget every scruple, every reservation, and be with this man.

"I'm sorry we were interrupted," she whispered.

"Me, too. Next time the coast is clear and you want to throw caution to the winds, I hope you call me." He paused, then added, "I really hope you call me."

He paused again. "Soon. Very, very soon."

Carly laughed. There was something about Chuck. He made her laugh. He made her feel…

That was it. He made her feel. But right now, she had her kids to think about. "When the coast is clear, I'll make that call."

He leaned down and gave her another quick buss. "I'll hold you to that."

He left. Carly peeked out the window and watched while he got in his car, then took a second to collect herself before she went into the kids. "So, what are we going to do tonight?"

"Who was that who just left?" Rhiana asked.

"A friend. He's in charge of the Safety Awareness Program. We talked about how my first two sessions went and how to improve next week's—"

"That's not all it was, though, right? Not just a business meeting?" Rhiana pressed.

"No." Carly wasn't sure how to answer. She didn't want to give the impression that Chuck was someone who would impact the kids' lives, because he wouldn't. She was going to do her best to see their paths didn't cross again. "We went out to a late lunch first. It's so busy at the schools that there's no time to eat. And seriously, even if there was, I don't do cafeteria food."

"Not me," Sean said. "I love it. Mystery-meat Mondays. Tuna-surprise Tuesdays…"

Rhiana wasn't going to get sidetracked at the thought of cafeteria food. She'd zoned in on Chuck and wouldn't be put off course. "Great. First Dad chooses his girlfriend over us, and now you're going to have a new guy, too."

"First, Chuck's not exactly my new guy. He's not the kind of guy I'd even remotely consider. And secondly, I would never, never ever pick someone else over you two. I may date in the future, but you guys are my priority. Always."

"Sure," Rhiana said.

Sean had been willing to discuss cafeteria food, but was totally silent about Chuck, which seemed worse to Carly. At least Rhiana was venting. Sean was holding in everything that mattered to him. Mystery meat was so much easier for him to talk about than the fact his parents had divorced. That worried Carly.

"Listen, I know things have changed for you two. Your dad and I split, I went back to school and got a job. And change is hard. It's hard for me, too. If I could build a perfect world for you, I would. But if I did, it would be a lie. Life isn't perfect, it's messy. Things happen. Good things. Crap things. You have to take whatever happens and make it work. That's all you can do."

"Yeah, you and Dad breaking up was crap." Sean glanced at her to see if she was going to yell about him using a normally forbidden word.

"You can say that again," Carly told him.

"Crap, crap, crap…" he chanted.

"Gee, Mom, way to go." Rhiana sounded exasperated, but a small smile played at the edge of her lips. "He's never going to stop saying it now."

"Crap, crap…"

"It's a limited time suspension of the rules," Carly clarified for Rhiana.

Sean stopped. "How limited?"

Carly glanced at her watch. "Two more minutes."

"Crap, crap…" he started chanting as quickly as possible.

What the heck, Carly thought, and still watching her watch, joined in, "Crap, crap, crap…"

Rhiana gave them both a you're-crazy look, but eventually, she gave in to temptation. "Crap, crap, crap…"

"Time's up," Carly announced when the two minutes had passed. "And just to be clear, that's it for that word, Sean."

"Next time Dad does something stupid can we have another crappy minute or two?"

Maybe a good mother, a proper mother, would never have started crappy minutes, but it had allowed Sean to vent. It had given all three of them a much-needed release.

"Yes. But I'm the Queen of Crappy Minutes, and I will decide when they're invoked."

"But we can request them?" Sean pressed.

"Come on, Sean, you're in seventh grade, not third," Rhiana complained.

"And I'm older than both of you, Rhi," Carly said. "And I can tell you, seventh grade or early thirties, everyone needs crappy minutes. And yes, Sean, you can request them."

"Okay."

For an instant, Carly thought he might hug her, but while Sean might not be too cool for crappy minutes, he was too cool to hug a mom. Good thing for him that Carly wasn't above hugging him. She leaned over and pulled both kids into her embrace. "I love you both. More than anything."

"Oh, gross. Mom germs. Ugh," Sean screamed.

"Maybe I'll get a camera and take pics of us all hugging. I could open a MySpace page."

"Oh, gee, Mom," Rhiana cried in horror. "You wouldn't?"

"Then I could 'friend' every kid from Erie Elementary and show off my pictures."

"Mom," they both cried in horror.

"Geesh, no sense of humor," she teased as she let them go.

Suddenly serious again, Rhiana asked, "Hey, what about poor Grandma?"

"Dad's such a dork," Sean muttered.

"We don't use that kind of language," Carly reminded him. "Well, not without express permission, and never about your father. Whatever he is, whatever he does, he's still your father. Nothing's going to change that. As for your grandmother, I was going to say we'd call tomorrow, but it's not even seven. Why don't you call tonight? That way you two can be the first to wish her a happy birthday."

"If Dad's not going to Cleveland, she's going to be all alone."

Carly shouldn't feel bad. They'd never been very close. Yet, she did sympathize.

No one should be all alone on their birthday. She mentally calculated everything she had to do over the weekend, and knew there weren't enough hours to get it all done no matter what, so what would blowing a few more hours matter? "Okay, here's what we'll do. If the weather's not bad, why don't you see if she wants to meet us in Mentor for lunch?"

Mentor, Ohio, was about halfway between Cleveland and Erie. Just a bit over an hour away.

"Really, Mom?" Rhiana asked.

"Sure. Why don't you call her and see if she wants to?"

Sean ran over to her and hugged her, all of his own volition. Rhiana followed suit. "Thanks," they chimed in unison and then sprinted away to find portable phones so they could both talk at once.

Carly could take her books and study while the kids spent time with their grandmother. Somehow she'd make it all work.

And what about Chuck?

Given what her days looked like, how was she ever going to find a moment for him…a moment she very much wanted to find?

Chapter Six

The following Friday, Chuck waited for Carly after what was their fourth Safety Awareness Program presentation. "Any chance you're open for dinner tonight?"

He hadn't really had a chance to talk to her on Tuesday. She'd hurried out because one of her kids was sick. He'd wanted to call. Really wanted to. But he hadn't. Mainly because he really wanted to.

He'd planned on playing it cool today, but obviously couldn't quite manage cool.

Carly smiled. "Wish I could. I have to pick up the kids, get them ready to go to their dad's. Dean's coming about seven. It's going to be quite the battle to get them to go because Rhiana hasn't forgiven him for last weekend. He called a few times this week, but she wouldn't talk to him. And though Sean did, he wasn't overly enthusiastic."

"I can't say that I blame them." A father who only had weekends with his kids, and would freely give up spending time with them in favor of a girlfriend…he didn't get that. Or a man who had a wife like Carly and would mess it up by cheating on her…he didn't get that either.

She shrugged. "I guess it's obvious to everyone that I never really understood Dean, but I really don't understand how cavalier he is about spending time with the kids." She took a deep breath, as if calming herself. "But I can't control what he does. Neither can Rhiana. She's going to have to learn that he's her father and she has to make peace with it. I keep telling her she can change her mind, can change her outfit, but she's stuck with the two of us as parents—warts and all."

Chuck snorted. "My mom always had those kinds of sayings. I bet that goes over well with Rhiana because I remember just how much I loved them."

Carly laughed. "About as good as when my mom used to tell me that sticks and stones… I always swore I wouldn't be that kind of mom, the one who throws meaningless platitudes at their kids. And yet, here I am. All my mother's sayings seem to tumble out of my mouth of their own accord. She'd have had a good laugh over it if she were still here."

"Losing her still hurts, doesn't it?"

"I miss her. Most of the time I forget how much, but when I came to dinner at your place and met your mom, it sort of hit me anew. I'd sort of hoped when I married that Dean's mother would kind of take me in. And though Darlene and I got along, it was never that close mother-daughter relationship I wanted. Your mom and I probably bonded over that one meal more than I ever did with Darlene."

"I think my mother would take that as a supreme compliment. I'm supposed to bring you back to dinner soon. Speaking of dinners, maybe we could do dinner tonight after your ex picks the kids up? Seven's not that late?"

He was pushing and he knew it, he just couldn't seem to stop himself.

"I have a PTA meeting, then I'm heading out to listen to a band we might book for the Valentine's dance. I'll confess,

I'm late getting started with planning it. I was going to let the kids use an iPod and speakers, but turns out this is an adult dance. Just what I wanted. Planning a night for a bunch of lovesick adults to moon over each other." She made a very unladylike gagging motion.

"Hey, you and me both. Valentine's is the bane of every single guy out there. Especially when avoiding a serious relationship is your credo. If you've been seeing a woman near the holiday, then you have to send them something. And if you do, they always read more into than you intended. I try not to date in February until after the fourteenth."

"Wow. You're a real Mr. Romance, Chuck."

He didn't take offense. It was the truth. "That's what they tell me. But about tonight… What if I came with you? We'll grab a bite, listen to the band and visit."

"There's never a good way to visit in a bar…they're awfully loud."

Chuck had been thinking about Carly all week. And seeing her at two of the safety programs wasn't enough. He'd tried to reposition the tables so she'd be close enough that they could chat between kids, but Firefighter Bob had nixed that, claiming that she should be closer to the firefighter's booth since she was handing out the fire-safety material. Watching Bob chat so amicably to Carly had been ulcer-producing.

Chuck wasn't a jealous guy, but there was something about "I-don't-poach" Firefighter Bob that set his teeth on edge. "Then we'll eat in the loud bar and save the visiting for after."

"By visit do you mean, *visit?*" Carly asked the question with just the right inflection so that he couldn't mistake her meaning.

"If you want me to mean *visit,* I certainly do, but I understand if the other night was a fluke." A fluke he wished hadn't been interrupted because all he'd been able to think about since was another chance at *visiting* with Carly Lewis.

"Then, yes. I'd love to have you come along with me and listen to the band. Afterward…" She shrugged. "We can see if either of us are interested in *visiting*."

Chuck was sure his interest in *visiting* with her wasn't going anywhere. He just hoped her interest in it was still there.

THAT NIGHT, AFTER GETTING the kids to go with Dean, Carly was the first one to arrive in the teachers' lounge where the PTA moms now held their meetings. It was a plain, but comfortable room. Tables, chairs, a fridge, microwave and phone. She put on a pot of coffee, then set out the napkin holder next to a plate of cannolis she'd bought at the International Bakery on her way to pick the kids up at school. She took one with chocolate filling as she sat and waited for Samantha and Michelle.

Samantha rushed in first. "Oh, man, cannoli. My life just gets better and better."

The coffeemaker made its last sputtering noises, indicating it had done its job. Carly got up and poured them each a cup. "So, tell me what else is ranking with the cannolis today."

Samantha shook her head as she studied the cannolis as if the fate of the world rested on her choosing the right one. She finally picked up a custard one. "Nope. I can't tell you my news till Michelle gets here."

"I'm here and the first thing I hear is my name," said their friend as she came up the short row of stairs and across the hall. "So, what can't you tell, Samantha?"

She took off her coat and made a beeline for the coffee. "Oh, cannoli," she practically purred.

"That's what I said," Samantha assured her and took a huge bite.

"Hey, quit eating long enough to tell us your news," Carly commanded.

After a day like today, she could use some good news.

Rhiana had been just as difficult about going with Dean as she'd anticipated. And rather than apologize and promise to do better, he'd greeted her surliness with an *Oh, grow up,* which was sure to make Rhiana even more cranky. "Chew, chew," Carly chanted. "We're waiting."

Samantha hurriedly chewed and swallowed her bite of cannoli, then took an agonizingly long sip of coffee.

"Samantha," Carly cried with the same impatience Rhiana might have used when dealing with Sean. She heard it in her own voice and recognized it, but couldn't help it. Samantha looked as if she were ready to burst with whatever news she had, and was being Seanesque, dragging it out for all it was worth. Next time Rhiana complained, she vowed to be more sympathetic.

Samantha looked totally unrepentant as she finally started. "I know we've all known each other for years, but this friendship…well it's new, even though it doesn't feel new. So, if you say no, I'll understand, but I'd really like you both to be bridesmaids when Harry and I get married…" She paused.

"Samantha," Michelle said this time.

"I can't help it, I want to savor the telling. We're getting married in June." Samantha didn't get any further than that. Both Carly and Michelle gave very girly shrieks, and hugged her.

When the commotion died down, Samantha finished. "Harry and I want the day to be filled with the special people in our lives. You were both here for me through the whole romance, and of all the people I know, I can't think of anyone I'd rather have be a part of this special day." She sniffed. "I swore I wouldn't do this."

She sniffed again and took one of the napkins next to the cannolis.

"Oh, Samantha, I'd be honored," Michelle cried.

Literally cried.

Tears streamed down Michelle's face. "I don't know what I'd have done without the two of you these last few months either. I don't think friendships like ours are forged with time, but with a connection. You two…" She gave up trying to talk and simply hugged Samantha all over again.

Carly could feel the tears tickling at the back of her eyelids.

She looked at the two women who'd been stuck on the Social Planning Committee with her. She remembered the morning Heidi had called and how annoyed she'd been to add one more thing to her list of things to do, but now, she realized that it had been one of the luckiest moments of her life. She wanted to say all that and more to Samantha and Michelle, but all she managed was, "Yes," before she gave in to the tears and joined the group hug.

When their tear-fest stopped, they all ate cannolis, drank their coffee and listened to Samantha's wedding plans. "…something simple. I've done the whole-nine-yards wedding, and it didn't take. This time, I want a simple celebration of the fact I love Harry and he loves me. I want family and friends there. Casual. So I don't have to worry about the kids messing up their clothes, or Stella's doll causing a table to catch on fire again."

Carly shook her head. "A simple celebration? There's no simple about what you and Harry have, and there will be no simple about the wedding. It sounds perfect."

Samantha looked at her watch. "I officially took up the whole meeting with wedding talk. Carly, about the Valentine's dance?"

"Everything's under control," she assured them as she glanced at the clock. "But, I'm going to have to run."

"I thought maybe we'd go out and celebrate," Samantha said. "Unless you have to get back to the kids."

"Daniel's keeping Brandon overnight," Michelle said. "So, I'm game."

Part of Carly wanted nothing more than to go celebrate Samantha's news with her friends. But she'd promised to meet Chuck, and truth be told, she'd been pretty much a fluttery mess since they'd agreed to meet and possibly *visit*.

"The kids are at Dean's tonight," she admitted. "But I'm supposed to go listen to a band I might book for the Valentine's dance."

"Great, we can come with you," Samantha said as Michelle nodded her agreement.

Carly squirmed. "I was meeting someone there, but you two are welcome to join us."

"Someone?" Samantha asked, a sly grin on her face. "Would this be a male someone by any chance? One who comes equipped with his very own handcuffs?"

"Oh, gross," Carly said.

"Is that an oh-gross about Samantha's very inappropriate handcuff comment, or oh-gross about the idea of dating a particular lieutenant?" Michelle grinned.

"The handcuffs," Carly assured her. "And the lieutenant is just meeting me to listen to this group."

"Great. Since it isn't a date, we'll just come along and listen, too." Samantha clapped her hands together. "It'll be like a double date—" she glanced at Carly and added "—that isn't a date."

Michelle shot Carly an I'm-sorry look. "If you're sure?"

There was no way out of it. First her kids. Now her friends.

Carly wondered if it was some kind of sign that she and Chuck weren't meant to *visit*.

She didn't say that to Michelle and Samantha. What she said was "Sounds good. It's a date."

DESPITE THE BAD WEATHER, Chuck was waiting for Carly on the street in front of her house at eight. He'd been waiting for fifteen minutes, not that he'd tell her that.

Carly pulled her van into the garage and hurried back out to his car. A gust of wind blew in as she opened the door.

"Heat," she gasped. "Crank it. I can't feel my feet."

He looked down at her very stylish black knee-high, huge-heeled boots. "Maybe you should have worn something warmer than those boots. Something more practical, too."

"Wearing anything with heels is practical when you're vertically challenged."

He laughed. "Vertically challenged?"

"Short. I can say it, but vertically challenged sounds better. And truly, a lot of short women have made their mark. Kristin Chenowyth is one of my all-time favorite actresses, both on stage, on TV and in film. And she's even tinier than me."

"Vertically challenged and in need of heels or not, you should still have something warmer on your feet."

"Thanks, Mom," she mocked.

Chuck sighed. "I've said this before, but you know, you're a very prickly woman, Carly Lewis."

"No. Not prickly. I'm simply firm about the fact I won't do what I'm told ever again. No matter what. I'll wear what-ever boots I want, even if my feet turn to ice."

"I'm not trying to tell you what to do…" He let the sentence trail off. "Okay, I was, but it was because I worry about you."

"If you're worried, then crank the heat so I can thaw my feet."

He obliged, turning the heating system on high.

Carly made a little sound of delight in the back of her throat. Soft, almost a sigh, it was the sound of a happy, satisfied woman.

"Oh, I've got my glee on now."

"Pardon?"

"Glee," she repeated slowly. "Bliss. Two very underused words."

"Okay, Miss Bliss, warm your feet while we drive to the club. I'll drop you off, then park and meet you inside."

"I can walk."

He glanced over, and could see her stubborn expression. "Carly, I know you can walk, and you will…from the car to the front door. I'm not telling you what to do, Miss Prickles. I'm telling you what I'm going to do. There's a difference."

"You're a stubborn man."

"Ah, it's rather one of those pot-calling-the-kettle things, now isn't it?" He stopped teasing and said, "But I'm glad this particular pot allowed this particular kettle to come out with her."

"About that."

There was something in her voice that sounded almost apologetic and made Chuck decidedly nervous. "Yes?"

"I need to apologize."

Good to know his cop senses hadn't totally deserted him with Carly Lewis. He was pretty sure an apology offered before any offense was taken was not a good thing—especially when Carly Lewis was involved. "About what? You haven't been playing with matches again?"

She laughed. "No matches or couches. But I do need to apologize about tonight. You see, it won't just be the two of us. We're sort of inadvertently double dating."

"What couple?"

"Not a couple in the traditional sense. The two moms on the PTA committee with me are coming along."

Ah, her friends. That wasn't so bad. From her apology, he'd thought it was going to be something worse. "Your friends are coming along to help you decide about the band."

"I could let you think so, and that's probably what they'd tell you, if you asked. Or they might tell you they came out to celebrate the fact Samantha and Harry have set a date for their wedding. But to be honest, they're coming to check you out."

"Oh?" It had been a long time since he'd been checked out by a date's friends. He didn't generally stick around long enough for it to get to that.

"I tried to explain that we're casual, but they're… Well, there's no way to be diplomatic. They're nosey. And since they've both found romance, they're convinced there's something magical about our committee and I'm going to find mine. I keep telling them I'm done with love and romance…the whole nine yards. But women in love don't listen well. I think their hearts get in the way of their ears. I just don't want you to worry that I'm getting the wrong idea. I'm not. And I don't want you to get the wrong idea and think I am."

She sounded emphatic.

Emphatically anti-romance.

That's exactly what Chuck wanted to hear from a woman he was dating, so those words should have made him happy. Although for some odd reason, they sort of rankled. "That's what you say now, but some day—"

"Chuck, what I'd love is for you not to tell me how I feel, or how I will feel. I lived with someone who tried to mold me into who they wanted me to be for too many years. I won't do it again—not even for a date."

"Sorry. It's just a woman like you should be loved." Chuck grimaced at the words. If any of the guys at the station had overheard that particular sentence they'd have never let him live it down.

Carly didn't seem to notice his momentary lapse into saccharine sentiments.

"I am loved. Loved by my kids. Loved by my friends. That's enough."

Chuck didn't say so, but he knew it shouldn't be enough. Carly deserved more than that.

He didn't say it. He knew she'd protest. So he simply pulled in front of the bar on State Street.

"Honestly, I can walk," she tried one more time.

He didn't even bother to respond. He simply waited until she sighed, got out of the car, and walked toward the entrance to the bar. Only then did he merge back into traffic and look for an empty meter. When he walked back to the bar, Carly was waiting inside the front door.

"You could have gone in without me. I'm a cop, remember? I'd have found you."

"I didn't mind waiting."

The bar was a popular weekend spot. They threaded their way through the crowd, and toward the back of the room Carly waved at two women in a booth against the wall. The brunette and tall blonde stood as they approached.

"Samantha, Michelle—" Carly indicated the shorter brunette was Samantha and the taller blonde was Michelle "—this is Lieutenant Jefferson."

"Chuck," he said. The woman scrutinized him for longer than might be polite. Chuck tried not to take offense. He liked that they were sizing him up in an attempt to look out for Carly.

He wondered if she bristled as much over their concern as she did his?

They all sat down. He noticed that Carly's friends had taken one side of the booth together, leaving the other side for Carly and himself.

"Carly and a cop…gotta confess, I didn't see that coming," Samantha said with a chuckle.

"There's no *and* about it," Carly said quickly. Too quickly. "There's Chuck. There's me. There's a few more Safety Awareness Program afternoons, and a band to listen to tonight. That's it."

"That's what I said about Harry. There was me. Him. And my boys in his office." She wiggled her ring finger. "And now look at us. We're getting married," she told Chuck. "A June wedding. Carly and Michelle are my bridesmaids…" The woman began to wax enthusiastic about her wedding plans.

Chuck tried to zone out, but Samantha's excitement was infectious. Carly shot him a look he interpreted as, "What else can I do?" as she joined in the planning.

"Pardon me," he said, and went to find the bartender and ordered a bottle of champagne.

He came back to the conversation, which still seemed to be centered on flowers. He sat back down and oohed and aahed on command until the bottle of champagne arrived.

"Chuck?" Carly asked, glancing at the glasses that the waiter had set down.

"Hey, it's not every day you get to celebrate a friend's happiness." He poured a glass for each of the four of them. "To Samantha and Harry. May you have a lifetime of happy years together."

They all toasted, and he added, "Thank you, ladies, for allowing me to crash your celebration."

"I'm afraid we're the ones crashing your date," Michelle admitted. She was by far the quietest of the three friends. "So, you're the one owed a thanks."

"Not every man could handle a night on the town with three women," Samantha said.

"Especially three women discussing wedding plans. I bet you wish you were anywhere but here." Carly gave him a look that said *she* wished she were any place but at a table talking about weddings. Weddings that she'd made abundantly clear she no longer believed in.

And that was the worst of it.

Chuck had no desire to pursue a wedding…but a woman like Carly should be part of a long-term partnership. The fact her ex had ruined her for that made him want to…

He was a cop, he couldn't even indulge thinking about what he'd like to do to Carly's ex. Still, even if neither of them was overly marriage-enthused, he, at least could go along with it for her friends' sakes. "Ladies, no man in his right mind wouldn't love to be where I am. A glass of champagne in my hand, and three lovely women for companionship. The guys at the station are going to be eating their hearts out when I tell them how I spent my weekend."

"Speaking of spending the weekend, I think the band's setting up now," Carly said.

The band, Landshark 4, got settled and started playing a bunch of Jimmy Buffet covers.

"What do you think?" Carly practically shouted to be heard over the music.

The other women nodded. "Maybe we could ask them to turn down the volume just a bit at the dance?" Michelle hollered back.

They all nodded their agreement as the song ended.

Chuck recognized the opening notes of "Son of a Son of a Sailor." "Speaking of dancing..." He stood and held out a hand. "Want to?"

Okay, so it wasn't the most eloquent invitation, but Carly's look of surprise seemed a bit much. "You do dance?" he asked.

"I didn't think you did," she admitted as he led her to the small square of open space that was already crowded with dancers.

"Now, why would you think I don't dance?"

"I don't know. It doesn't seem very macho. I mean, when I think cops, I think guns drawn, kicking in the door and taking down the...perps?"

He laughed. "Call me a renaissance man because I can draw a weapon, and lead a pretty woman around on the dance floor."

They stopped talking and Chuck just held her. Despite her crazy high heels, she moved smoothly on the dance floor, picking up and following his rhythm. He liked the way she felt against him. The top of her head barely reached his shoulder, so she snuggled a cheek into his chest.

"So, is this our song?" Chuck asked, joking.

Carly must not have noticed the humor in his question because he could feel her body get all tense.

"Chuck, we won't be together long enough to have a song, remember?"

He should probably kick himself for asking something like that. It broke all his keep-things-light rules. Instead of backtracking, he said, "Whether we're together or not, we can have a song. Tell you what, every time I hear Jimmy Buffet, I'll think of you."

"Oh, so we won't have a song, we'll have the *whole* singer?" Her tone was light, but her body was still rigid in his arms.

"Hey, I like you…what can I say? Some women might only warrant a song, but you, Carly, you deserve a prolific singer."

She didn't just relax, she sort of melted into him. "I think that's one of the nicest things anyone's said to me in years." She paused and added, "And I guarantee that I will think about you, about this, every time I hear Buffet. I'm no Parrothead, but I have a number of his CDs and go to the tribute concert each year on the bayfront."

They didn't talk any more after that…they didn't need to. Even when the band switched to a faster song, they continued dancing, swaying to a beat it felt as if only they were following.

Chapter Seven

Carly counted. They'd been dancing for four songs.

She glanced over at the table. Michelle and Samantha were watching them with a particular gleam in their eyes that made her nervous. "Chuck, we should probably get back to my friends."

"You're right. But afterward, when I take you home…" He didn't finish the sentence.

Carly didn't need him to.

For the first time in years, she knew what she wanted.

Not what she should want.

Not what someone else wanted her to want.

Simply what she wanted.

And what she wanted was Chuck. "Yes, afterward."

The rest of the evening was a blur. She knew she conversed with Samantha and Michelle, but, if asked, she wouldn't have been able to pinpoint one single topic of that discussion. All she could think about was Chuck, about what she'd practically promised was going to happen when they went home.

And she did want him, but—

It was that darned *but* that was getting in the way. She

wanted to be carefree and go-with-the-flow. She wanted to be the kind of woman who could enter into a casual relationship with a man. That's what she wanted.

But.

But, in actuality, she'd never been in a casual relationship. Before Dean, she'd had boyfriends, but she'd been so young, she'd fallen head over heels for each, thinking the high-school love would last forever. Dean was her first serious college boyfriend and that had lasted right up to the moment she'd signed the divorce papers.

With Chuck there was no talk of ever-afters. No telling herself that she'd be intimate with him because she loved him. And to be honest, she wasn't sure how to do that—how to have a physical relationship that involved a whole lot of like, but no talk of love.

When the band finished their set, she went to talk to them, telling them they had the dance if they wanted it.

Then she went back to the table, and they said good-night to Samantha and Michelle. "Congrats again," she told Samantha as she hugged her friend.

"Have fun tonight," Samantha whispered. "You two were practically burning up that dance floor."

That comment made her nervous as well.

"You're quiet," Chuck said as they drove to her house.

"Sorry. Just thinking."

"I could play dumb and ask about what, but I won't. We don't have to do anything you don't want to do."

Chuck was sweet. He probably would hate to hear that description as much as she suspected he'd hate to hear about his cuteness, but there it was. Lieutenant Chuck Jefferson was sweet and cute.

And that innate sweetness was why she knew he meant what

he said. And it was the reason she wanted to do what was making her nervous. "Oh, I do want to. I just don't know *how* to."

"You have two kids," he pointed out, "so I assume you know *how* to."

Carly was glad it was late. It was somehow easier having this conversation while he was driving in the dark and couldn't see her. "But I was with someone I thought I loved, someone I thought loved me. With you, there's only physical need. And I don't want to minimize that need, because it's big and getting bigger by the minute. It's that I don't know how to do that."

"I can show you…if you want. But only if you want. I'm not into meaningless sex. I don't want to make it sound that way. There has to be a connection between us, or it doesn't work. I just don't try to pretty it up and call it love. I think we have that connection, Carly. And you have to feel it, too."

Carly knew offering her an out wasn't simply a way for him to call it off. She might have been removed from the dating game for a while, but she could tell he genuinely wanted her. No, this was Chuck being a nice guy and giving her an opportunity to change her mind. He didn't love her, but he cared enough not to force her into something she might regret. He was right, there was a connection here.

That thought warmed her and helped solidify in her mind what she wanted. "Chuck, I may not know how to have a relationship with a man who has no emotional ties with me, but I'd very much like to…with you."

"Phew. Being a nice guy was killing me."

"We wouldn't want that." She put her hand on his thigh. Nothing more. She didn't move it to any more risqué locations. His thigh was enough to make her feel brazen. She noticed he sped up a bit; moments later they pulled up in her drive and hurried into the house, laughing like two kids.

Purposefully, she locked the door and was slipping the chain in place as Chuck came up behind her and nuzzled on her neck. "You're sure the kids aren't coming home?"

The door locked, she turned around into Chuck's embrace. "As sure as I can be."

"Well then—" He pulled her close and kissed her.

Carly could feel his very real desire. She'd heard the word *hungry* used, and it fit here. He was hungry for her, which was good since she felt the same. It was almost a pressure, building, pulling her closer. She knew if they could just get close enough, that pressure would ease.

She pulled off her coat, hat and scarf, again without breaking off their kiss and dropped them to the floor. Chuck followed suit.

Reminiscent of their last aborted attempt.

"I think, last time, we made it as far as my room. Maybe this time we could make it to the bed?"

He released her, took her hand and immediately started up the stairs. "You don't have to ask me twice."

She laughed as she ran behind him.

"Right one?" he asked, opening the door and pulling her inside.

Carly ran for the bed, jumped in the center and toed off her boots. "Hurry, on the bed. We'll officially have gone farther than last time."

Chuck jumped next to her, they bounced and both laughed. Fun.

Being with Chuck was fun. Easy. Maybe that's what coming into something casual meant…it could just be fun and easy.

As they stopped playing and started kissing again, an overwhelming feeling of rightness came over Carly.

"Carly, I—" His cell phone rang, interrupting whatever he was going to say. "Sorry, let me check."

He fished the phone out of his pocket. "I have to take this."

He stepped out into the hall. She could hear his murmured responses to whoever had called.

She felt awkward. At least when her kids had interrupted she'd had something to do. Now she had to sit in the middle of her bed with her clothing askew, trying not to listen to Chuck's conversation.

She raised her hand and ran a finger lightly over her lips. She felt aware of them. It's not that she didn't always know she had lips—she did. But didn't often give them much thought. They were just there. She used them when she ate and when she talked, but really, even then she didn't pay much attention to them.

Now, they tingled a bit, leaving her very much aware that they were there and that recently they'd been thoroughly kissed.

When Chuck re-entered the room and turned his attention to other parts of her body, would they come as alive for her?

She found she was anxious to find out.

Chuck walked into the room, but this time there was no laughter as he jumped on her bed. There wasn't even a trace of a smile. "Carly, I so hate to do this to you—hell, to me, too. But I've got to go."

"Pardon?" Her fingers dropped from her lips and she was back to sitting awkward on her bed, clothing askew.

"That was the station. There's been a major drug bust. I've got to go. The Chief wants me there to deal with the press, and there's going to be press. It's my job."

"Oh." An excuse. Dean had millions of those. *Carly, I have to work late. This is a big case. Carly, I'm going to dinner with the partners and some other people from the office. I'll be home soon.*

She'd never thought anything of them until she'd caught

him with his secretary, and then she questioned every late night, every weekend away, everything.

And as Chuck straightened his clothing, she questioned his excuse. Not that she thought he had another woman on the side, but maybe he'd finally discovered whatever it was about her that had driven Dean away. He was kissing her, and then was saved by the bell…well, phone.

"Carly, look I'm sorry. Looks like the universe is against us. Your kids, my job. I promise we'll figure it out. Maybe I could come back afterward and—"

"Hey, don't worry about it. No strings, remember? I have kids, you have the department. Neither of us wants anything but short-term and casual, so there are no recriminations. Go do what you need to. I'll probably be asleep before you're done."

"Can I call you tomorrow?"

"Sure. I have errands and will be in and out all day, but yes, call."

He leaned down and kissed her again. Not a tingle-producing kiss, but rather a very perfunctory peck on the lips. "Tomorrow. I'll call."

"Great."

She escorted him to the front door and willed herself not to peek out the window and watch him pull out of the drive.

Casual. Short-term. That's all this was. He had to work. There was nothing sinister in that.

However, a small voice whispered in her ear, wondering if that was the last she'd see of Chuck Jefferson. And as she realized what she'd just thought, she got mad.

Not at Chuck for leaving.

Not at the police station or her kids for interrupting them.

At herself for being so willing to accept that there was something wrong with her.

There was nothing wrong with her.

Dean was a skunk.

Her kids needed her.

Chuck had a job. Chuck wanted her, but he had something unavoidable to do.

She could sit in her bedroom feeling sorry for herself. Or she could be proactive. She could acknowledge that she and Chuck both had priorities, and try to figure out some way around them.

CHUCK SPENT MOST OF the night kicking himself and wondering why he had ever thought becoming the voice of the police department was a good idea.

He'd wanted to head back to Carly's after he finished up at the station, but she'd sort of made it clear that she intended to be sleeping.

"Last night was only another indication of why cops shouldn't get involved with women. When work calls, even if it is a Friday night and you have plans, you have to go. And the woman in question gets pissed," he said to Anderson the next morning as they sat at George's sipping coffee and waiting for their breakfasts.

"What did you do?"

"Carly and I were—" he was gentleman enough not to say exactly what they were doing "—out last night when I got called into work. I think Carly's mad. I don't blame her. I left her rather high and dry."

"Flowers. Send flowers. Women love that kind of thing."

"It's a bit of a cliché, don't you think?" He tried to picture himself handing Carly a bouquet and couldn't quite manage it. She'd probably fling the flowers right back at him. "I know she's rather biased against anything that's a cliché."

"Sleeping alone in your bed is cliché, too. Guess which cliché I'd pick?"

"You have a point. I could order some—" Chuck's phone rang. He fished in his pocket for it and muttered, "Seriously, tell me why I took this job again?"

But when he pulled it out and checked the caller ID, it wasn't a work number, it was Carly.

"Carly," he said by way of greeting.

Anderson raised an eyebrow and cocked his head to one side.

"Hey. Do you have a minute?" he heard her say. "I mean, if you're busy, you can call me back."

"Sure, I've got a minute." He held up a finger to Anderson, indicating he'd return in a momentarily, and walked toward the door, phone in hand. "About last night," he started.

"I'm not calling about last night. I'm calling about tonight. Can you get away?"

He stepped out into a bitter January wind blowing straight up State Street.

"I've got another Neighborhood Watch meeting I have to attend, but I should be out of there by sevenish at the latest."

"And after?" she pressed.

"I'm thoroughly at your disposal. What do you have in mind?" He felt warm, despite the cold, thinking about all the options he wouldn't mind her naming.

No, not warm. Almost hot.

"A surprise." Her laughter heated him up even more.

"I'll pick you up around seven," she continued.

"And is this a put-on-a-suit surprise, or a come-in-jeans surprise?" Not that he cared. He just wanted to spend time with Carly, didn't matter the circumstances.

"It's a pack-an-overnight-bag surprise."

He gave her his address, then the significance of her words sank in. "Oh… Oh, how did you manage—"

"No questions now, or you'll ruin the surprise. Pack an overnight bag, and maybe tell everyone at work you might be out of touch for a while tonight."

"How long is a while?"

"I suppose that's going to depend on…" She hesitated. He could almost hear her smile over the phone. "On your stamina."

"I'll be sure to let everyone know not to call unless it's an absolute emergency, if that's the case, because my stamina is legendary."

"Hey, that's big talk, buddy. I'm hoping you can back it up."

"Don't you mean keep it up?"

"Okay, okay, this conversation is getting a bit risqué. Tell me you're alone at home?"

"Actually, I'm at George's having breakfast with Anderson."

"Ack. Hang up then and find a good excuse for this conversation. One that doesn't involve me. Oh, can you imagine how he'd torture me? Tell him you were talking to a perp, a reporter…I don't care who you tell him it is, just don't tell him it's me."

Chuck didn't mention he was standing outside freezing because he'd wanted to steal some time alone with her…even if it meant standing in a foot of snow. "I'll think of something."

"I'll be at your house about seven-thirty." She hung up.

He hurried inside and found Anderson already chowing down on his eggs. Chuck gratefully picked up his coffee cup, willing his hands to regain some feeling.

"So, are you going to tell me? Do you need those flowers?" Anderson asked.

Chuck shook his head. "No, I don't think I do."

"Seriously? She forgave you that easily? I remember most of your exes did nothing but complain about your weird hours."

"She didn't even mention last night. She wanted to make some plans for tonight."

The waitress stopped at the table with a coffeepot in her hand. "Fill 'er up?"

Chuck set the coffee cup down. "Please."

Feeling a little warmer, he started his breakfast. Anderson didn't ask any other questions. Didn't press. That was one of the nice things about his brother-in-law. But Chuck wasn't really thinking about Anderson's consideration. His mind was on Carly and her surprise…her surprise that involved an overnight bag.

CARLY WAS A MASS of nerves by the time she pulled up in front of Chuck's that night. Not a bad, maybe-she-shouldn't-be-doing-this, self-doubt case of nerves. Rather a sort of fluttery nervous excitement.

She wanted Chuck.

After her initial disappointment, she'd understood that he'd had to leave last night, because it was the nature of his job. If she stayed at the hospital after she passed her boards, her hours would be just as crazy.

She wished she'd told him to come back over when he was done…whenever he was done.

She hadn't though, which was why she'd spent her night tossing and turning. When she finally did manage to doze off, her dreams had been full of Chuck, and what they might have done.

What they would do tonight, if she had her way.

She was relieved to see his car in the drive. She didn't have time even to get out of the car before his front door opened and he rushed toward her, overnight bag in hand.

"So?" he said as he climbed into the passenger seat. "What are we doing that involves an overnight bag? And don't try to hold me off with your ambiguous it's-a-surprise comments. I'm a cop. I know interrogation techniques and I'm not afraid to use them."

His teasing helped calm her nerves. She put the car in Reverse, and pulled out onto the street. "Well, I was doing some thinking—"

"It's always dangerous to hear you've been thinking, Carly Lewis. But I'm a cop and I live for danger, so go on."

Carly turned off 38th Street and headed north on State. Normally, she'd have noticed that today's wet snow had left all the trees coated. It looked beautiful in the moonlight. But tonight it was only a passing thought. All she could concentrate on was the fact that Chuck was sitting next to her, that she wanted him and that she wasn't waiting for fate. She was making it happen.

"I was thinking," she repeated. "If we wait for my kids and your work to give us a break, we'll never have sex. We'll reach the end of our fling without ever having flung. And that is a sad state of affairs…pardon my pun."

He chuckled. "And rhyme. Both were equally bad. I admit you've got a point and we wouldn't want that. *I* wouldn't want that."

"Well, once, I might have thrown up my hands and said that there was nothing I could do about a flingless fling. But after my divorce…" Oh, bad form to mention a divorce— which brought the existence of an ex into the conversation— when you were about to proposition a man. Carly wasn't sure she was ever going to get the hang of dating. "Sorry."

"About what? You were talking about flinging, and there's nothing to be sorry about there."

Thank goodness the light was green. She didn't want to waste any of their time together idling at red lights. She needed to be in Chuck's arms now.

"Carly?" he prompted. "You were talking about flinging?"

"Sorry. Thinking about flinging makes my mind wander. As I was saying, I decided I was done being anyone's doormat. I'm done waiting for life to offer me what I want. No one, not even fate, is going to tell me what to do. I realized it's up to me to reach out and take what I want."

"You can reach out and take me whenever you want."

"That's the plan. Tonight. Dean has the kids. So, it's just us."

"We're not heading to your house, though."

She continued to hit green lights as they traveled down State Street. "Oh, no, that was part of the planning. People know where I live, and we've already proven that's not good. I thought about suggesting we fling at your house, but people know where you live as well. They know your car, too, which is a bad thing since your cop buddies are everywhere in the city. That's why we're in my car and we're heading someplace they'll never find us."

"Where?"

"That's the surprise."

She turned and headed west on the Bayfront Highway, and in short order, turned onto the road that led to the new Convention Center. Carly pulled onto the parking ramp next to the hotel. "This is a perfect plan. I booked us at the hotel. Beautiful views, great ambiance. And as an added security measure, my car will be hidden in the ramp. We should be hard to track down."

"I like how you think." They got out of the car, and both grabbed their overnight bags from the backseat.

He reached out to take hers. Carly tugged it away from him. "I've got it."

And because that sounded a bit sharp, she added, "I want you to save your strength for tonight."

Chuck didn't argue, but he did slip his arm over her shoulders and brought her close.

Carly relished his touch. It had been so long since she'd felt like this. She leaned into him. He felt solid. A guy she could trust.

The walked briskly into the hotel and through the lobby without even stopping to notice the beautiful ambiance.

"Do we need to check in?" he asked as she bypassed the reservation desk.

Carly pulled their keycard out of her pocket. "Got it covered."

"You really did work at this."

The appreciation in his voice warmed her. "When I do something, I don't like to do it halfway. I came down early, checked in and scoped out the room. You're going to love it."

He jabbed the button for the elevator. "I've never been in here. The hotel's gorgeous. And you know that I'm only commenting on the decor because I'm trying to concentrate on behaving like a civilized man until we're someplace private."

The elevator doors slid open.

"Just how uncivilized are you planning to be, then?"

They entered the elevator and Carly pushed a button.

"As uncivilized as you'll let me," he assured her as the doors slid shut.

Carly turned to him and kissed him. It wasn't as long or

as deep as she'd have liked to make it, but she wanted to make her intentions very, very clear. And she settled for a brief reminder.

It must have been enough because Chuck whispered, "Wow," as the doors slid open.

She led him down the hallway. "You let work know you might not be answering your cell phone for a while?" she checked.

"I let them know. I told them I was going to be out of touch for the night. If they called, they could leave a message."

The fact that he'd do that, that he'd put his work aside for her, only added to the need Carly felt. She stopped in front of the farthest room. "Here we go."

She opened it. Closed the door behind them and bolted it shut. "Come look at this." She led him across the room to the floor-to-ceiling windows that overlooked the bay. The moon was full and bright, illuminating the entire frozen surface in a bluish light. "I could stay here all night looking out this window."

He stood behind her and wrapped his arms around her waist. "It is beautiful, but I'm hoping I can convince you to pull yourself away for a while. Because there's another scenic location I'd like to explore."

Without breaking his embrace, she turned so that she was facing him. "Scenic?"

"Very scenic." He nuzzled her neck.

"Before we both start sightseeing, I need to tell you that I'm not nervous about this." As she said the words she thought they sounded stupid, but she needed to say them.

"I'm glad." He continued kissing her neck, moving lower to her collarbone.

She couldn't remember ever having had her collarbone

kissed before. And if she'd thought about it, she wouldn't have imagined it would be sexy, but it was…incredibly sexy.

Carly forced herself to concentrate, to get out the words she needed to say before they went any farther. "Samantha was nervous. She hadn't made love to anyone other than her ex, and she was nervous about what Harry would think of her post-pregnancy body. I won't let that bother me."

"You don't need to let it bother you," he assured her, and gently unbuttoned just one small button on her blouse, his lips moving to below her collarbone, toward the little bit of cleavage she had.

"You're right, I don't. So, I have a few stretch marks? I won't let myself worry that you'll find them offensive."

Carly had to admit, Chuck didn't seem to be offended by anything. He gently undid one more button and caressed her with his lips.

She forgot what she'd been saying. Forgot to remember she wasn't nervous. She was simply lost in the feel of the man, the sensations he was evoking.

He didn't offer any more reassurances, but simply pulled her toward the bed.

"I'm okay with who I am, and if you're not—"

He gave a little nudge and she fell backward on the bed. He was immediately next to her. "Carly. I'm fine with you, fine with who you are. Fine with stretch marks. I'm sure I'll love your stretch marks, but first, you have to stop warning me so I can start."

"I just want—"

He pulled her into his arms. "You're nervous, despite your bravado." As he spoke, his breath brushed softly against her neck. "I get that. Guys get nervous, too. But you don't have to be anxious with me. I want you. Woman, I want you more than anyone…ever. I want to strip your clothes off you, slowly, one item at a time. And when you're naked, I want to trace every line, every curve, every stretch mark and memorize them. I want to…"

He unbuttoned another button and went back to exploring her body with his lips, slowly teasing all worries, all thought, from her as she lay back on the bed and let Chuck explore her body in his slow, seductive, tantalizing way.

A pressure began growing in her. Expanding as her need grew. Not just need. A need for Chuck.

Her clothes were long since gone, one at a time, as he'd promised. They now littered the floor, while Chuck was still fully clothed.

She sat up. "We have a problem."

"Your kids aren't here, my phone's turned off. What sort of problem could we have?"

She reached for his belt buckle and began working it loose. "You have way too many clothes on, and I—"

She didn't get to slowly and seductively strip him, as he'd stripped her. Chuck was up off the bed taking off his clothes faster than anything she'd ever witnessed. She smiled at the site of him.

She'd thought of him as cute, but now she acknowledged he was beautiful. She didn't say that to him. She didn't imagine his cop's pride would appreciate the sentiment, but he was absolutely, utterly beautiful to her.

"That's better," she assured him and reached for his hand, then pulled him down next to her. "So, where were we?"

"I was exploring." He gave her a nudge, as if he planned to continue.

"Sorry, buddy. Turn about's fair play." Carly needed to take control. Needed to set the pace.

She gave him a little shove back onto the bed. "Just stay still and let me have my way with you."

"Carly, you can have me whatever way you want."

Loving the feeling of freedom, Carly began her own exploration.

And what she found was worth the wait.

Chapter Eight

Carly woke up the next morning to the sound of knocking.

She felt a spurt of panic. She'd overslept and the kids were going to be late to school, and of course, she'd be late to work and…

She felt something warm on her left.

Chuck.

No one was late for work or school. It was the kids' weekend with their dad. It was Sunday morning and she was exactly where she was supposed to be.

She pried her eyes open and saw a strange ceiling. Slowly, she looked down and slowly lifted the covers. Yep, they were both still naked in a hotel together.

She'd forgotten all about the knock on the door as she enjoyed her new favorite view.

Chuck moved, and she forced her gaze from under the covers to meet his eyes.

"Uh, Carly, what are you doing?" he asked with a grin.

"Ogling you," she informed him, without making any attempt to alter her view.

"Ogling?" He repeated the word as if it were foreign.

"Yes, sir, I believe *ogling* is indeed the best word to

describe what I'm doing. It's a very nice view down here," she added. "I'd like to discuss our day's plans with you."

"Do we have plans?"

"Well, I think we should start our day by asking for a late checkout and then—" Someone knocked on the door again, reminding her of what had woken her up in the first place and interrupting her plans, all of which involved staying in bed.

"Who do you think that is? No one knows we're here, right?" Chuck checked.

"It's probably room service. I left an order for breakfast last night." She scrambled out of bed, found her bathrobe on top of her bag, and raced to the door, snatching her purse and grabbing a tip from her wallet.

She cracked open the door, and held out the bills. "You can just leave it there. I'll get it," she said, very aware of the fact there was a naked man in her bed.

"Thanks, ma'am."

She waited until the bellman had disappeared down the hall before she opened the door all the way and wheeled the cart into the room. She pushed it toward the bed and Chuck. "Breakfast in bed?"

"Only if afterward we can have some dessert." Chuck wiggled his eyebrows in such a way that Carly was absolutely sure what dessert he had in mind.

"Really? After all those times last night, you still want to…" She wiggled her own eyebrows and climbed back into the bed.

"I still want to. Carly, I can't imagine ever not wanting to with you."

She reached for a plate, but Chuck said, "Don't you dare start eating that yet."

Her hand froze. "What's wrong?"

"I believe you've got too many clothes on." He tsked.

"I only have my robe… Oh." She hesitated. "I've never eaten naked before."

Chuck laughed. "Neither have I. Let's both give it a shot and see what we think."

An hour and a half later, Carly decided that eating naked was her second new favorite thing to do.

Her first favorite thing was also done naked, but didn't involve croissants…it involved Chuck.

THEY SPENT THE WHOLE morning in bed.

It was a new experience for Chuck, one he'd have never considered before Carly.

It wasn't as if they made love all morning. They ate their breakfast, then read the newspaper that had accompanied their tray. Together, with coffees in hand, trading off sections amicably.

They'd made love again, then napped until it was time to check out.

Chuck could have made a plausible exit then. Normally he would have. But he wasn't ready to say goodbye to Carly just yet. Instead he changed the checkout time and ordered up lunch.

They should have run out of conversational topics. They'd been in each other's company for almost twenty-four hours, and yet they didn't. And when lunch was finished, he still wasn't ready to leave her.

If it had been warmer, he'd have suggested a walk along the bayfront, but it was a cold, blustery day. They'd packed up their overnight bags, and Carly stood, taking in one last look out their window. He stepped behind her, and as he'd done last night, wrapped his arms around her.

"Isn't it a beautiful view?"

It was a solid sheet of ice. Small ice-fishing huts broke up the whiteness. He could see the snow-covered trees across the bay on the peninsula.

He knew that was the view Carly was referring to, but he purposely looked at her as he responded, "Yes, it is."

She pressed her arms against his, tightening his embrace around her.

"I hate to leave," she admitted.

"Why don't I come back with you?"

"That wasn't a hint," she assured him. "We've been together since last night. I figured you'd had enough of me."

Part of him wanted to say he couldn't imagine ever having enough of Carly, but it sounded schmultzy even in his head, so he opted for, "Not yet."

"But you'll let me know when you have?"

He kissed her. "I don't think there's any worries about that."

"At least not for six weeks."

He studied her, but didn't see any signs of sarcasm, instead, there was humor in her eyes. He grabbed her, took her in his arms and nuzzled at her neck. "Six weeks is not a hard and fast rule, it's merely the way these things have tended to play out in the past. There are no rules for us," he repeated. And if there were, he suspected Carly wouldn't fit nicely within their confines.

Carly wasn't the type of woman to be constrained by rules.

She laughed. "I wasn't complaining, Chuck. To be honest, there's a comfort in knowing there's an end-date in sight. It makes you the perfect boy-toy."

"I'm a lieutenant on the police force," he huffed. "I'm no boy-toy."

"Chuck's a boy-toy, Chuck's a boy-toy," she taunted with a playground lilt to her chant. "You've confessed that that's the way you like it. Own your toyness, Chuck. Don't try to hide from it. Embrace your inner toyness."

"Funny." He tried to look serious, but couldn't quite pull it off in the face of her hilarity.

"Be the master of your toymain." She paused. "Get it? Domain…toymain?"

"Wow, that's bad, Lewis."

"Don't be coy, be a toy." She laughed, cracking herself up with her own silliness.

"Carly." He couldn't help but laugh, too.

"That's it, I'm out of toy comments."

"Good. Now, how about me going home with you?"

"The kids will be there around three."

"Fine. Let's go to your house then and wait for them. Afterward, what if I take you all out to eat? Another day of no cooking. That's always a good thing in my mother's eyes."

"Don't you have to be at your mother's? It's Sunday."

"I canceled yesterday. I said I had to work." Before she could tease him about lying, he added, "Do not comment, I'll state for the record, I did in fact work very hard."

"Chuck." Carly was suddenly all seriousness. She reached up and touched his cheek. "I don't want you to take this the wrong way, but no. My kids have been through enough. I'm not going to introduce them to a…" She hesitated.

"Boy-toy?" He tried to keep the bitterness out of his voice, but wasn't sure he managed.

"Boy-toy in the nicest way, Chuck. You're not sticking around. We both went into this relationship—and I use that word in the very broadest sense—knowing that. I don't think it's a good idea to confuse them, to introduce another man into their lives who will be leaving eventually."

"Don't introduce me as your boy-toy then." It had started off as a funny joke, but Chuck had to admit, the term was quickly losing some of its humor for him. "I'm just the cop you're working with on the safety stuff. Nothing more as far as they're concerned."

"It would be easier if I continued to keep my two lives separate."

"Carly, I don't want to make your life more difficult. I also don't want to go home without you. And I'd like to spend time with you and your kids, Carly. So, come on. Two volunteers sharing a meal with your kids. And you don't have to cook."

"Now, that is a true temptation," she admitted. "Not that I don't like to cook."

"You do?"

"It sort of goes hand-in-hand with the whole crafty thing. There's nothing like having a new cookbook, a new recipe. I'm a huge fan of *Cooking Light* magazine, and *Taste of Home*. And let's not even get started on my obsession with kitchen gadgets. They make my little heart go all aflutter."

"You are an interesting woman, Carly Lewis."

"I have unimagined depths."

He laughed. "Yes, you do. So, about this afternoon?" He kissed her neck again and she sighed twice.

"Fine. You win. But none of this hanky-panky in front of the kids. We're two professional associates sharing a meal and planning for our last two safety gigs."

He stopped in mid nibble and asked, "What time are the kids home?"

"Three."

"And what time do we have to be out of here?"

"The late checkout time is two."

He looked at his watch. "That leaves us fifty minutes. I think we should take total advantage of every minute we have here."

"Oh, do you, lieutenant?"

"Yes." Chuck had barely gotten the word out of his mouth, when Carly took control and saw to it they used every minute they had left as wisely as possible.

AT TEN TO THREE, Carly dropped Chuck off at his house so he could pick up his own car, then follow her to her place. Inside, as he hung up his coat, she just enjoyed the view for a moment. He was wearing a pair of charcoal pants and a nicely fitted black crewneck sweater.

It wasn't a fancy outfit, by any means, but it hugged his body, reminding her that she knew that body intimately now. Images from last night left her feeling slightly breathless.

"Carly?"

She was standing there ogling him again. "Uh, I've got to run this bag upstairs before the kids come home. I don't want any questions."

She needed to get the images from last night out of her mind before the kids were there, so she paused before sprinting up the stairs. "I know it's not in the good-hostess hand-book, but do you mind if I start a load of clothes? Weekends are my only time to catch up, and this weekend? Well, I've been otherwise occupied."

Laundry. Laundry was generally as antierotic as things came, but even thinking of dirty clothes wasn't enough to totally erase the images that kept replaying in her mind.

"I'll confess, I'm happy to occupy you that way anytime you say."

Great. That wasn't helpful in the least.

"Listen, as for the laundry, I invited myself over. You do what you need to."

Doing what she needed to? Or what she wanted to? Because what she wanted to…

Laundry. Think about the laundry.

"Great. Thanks. Make yourself at home."

CHUCK WASN'T SURE what was up with Carly, but he knew that he wished they hadn't had to leave the hotel. He could have spent the whole day there with her and still not been satisfied.

He wasn't sure what to do with himself while he waited for her, so he sat on the couch and picked up a *Country Living* magazine. He smiled as he thumbed through the dog-eared pages. He wondered if these were things Carly wanted to buy or make.

He noticed the file that had been underneath the magazine. It was marked Valentine's dance in a bold neon-green marker.

He opened it and found a very neat to-do list. The band was checked off.

Food. She had notes about the food.

Security. Did she need security for the thing? Valentine's was barely under a month away. Chuck didn't normally make plans that far in advance with any woman.

Carly arrived, bearing the basket of dirty clothes. "Thanks. I told Rhiana she was on her own for laundry, but I've already caved. Well, insofar as if it's in the laundry room, I'll wash it. I've got to start Sean's clothes first. It takes a little longer with his stuff since so much of it needs to be pretreated, and even occasionally post-treated. It amazes me how he manages to find dirt even in the middle of winter when the entire city is covered by at least a foot of snow."

Chuck held up the paper. "I was looking at your magazine and found your file and noticed your Valentine's dance list had security on it. Do you need someone?"

"Yes. It's school policy that any large gatherings must

have security. And since the proceeds from the dance are a fund-raiser, they're hoping for a big crowd. Do you know a cop who moonlights cheap?"

"I have a guy in mind. His going rate is a dance with a certain committee chair." He waited for the cold sweats to start as he voluntarily made plans for weeks in advance. They didn't come. But Carly looked as if she might have caught them, though.

She shook her head. "Chuck, you don't have to—"

"Hey, I went to a private school. I know it's against the school handbook to turn down volunteers."

"Well, it's just under a month away. And given the fluidity of our relationship…?" She looked as if she were going to argue more, then simply shrugged. "You're sure?"

"Positive." He picked up the pen next to the folder and checked off Security. "Is one officer enough?"

"I think that one will be fine. The school parents tend to be a quiet bunch."

"Hey, I met your friends and *quiet* isn't quite the word I'd use," he teased.

"They're a bit protective."

She didn't get any further because the front door opened. "Hey, Mom, we're home. Dad wants to talk to you," a girl who had to be Carly's daughter, Rhiana, called as she ran into the living room. "Oh, you have company."

A boy, who must be Sean, followed on his sister's heels. "Who's the guy?"

"Rhiana, Sean, this is Lieutenant Jefferson. I'm working with him on the safety program, and he's just volunteered to help out with the Valentine's Dance."

Chuck heard the front door close and Dean—very neatly pressed—came in the room. "Carly, we need to talk about…"

His sentence trailed off when he spotted Chuck. For a split second he froze.

Chuck couldn't decide if Dean was in shock, or merely assessing him. Chuck got up off the couch and walked over to him. His movement seemed to unfreeze the man.

Carly's ex nodded. "Hi, again."

"Lieutenant Chuck Jefferson. A good friend of Carly's."

That gave the man pause. "How good?"

Carly walked over and stood next to them. "Hey, kids, go take your stuff up to your rooms, okay?" She waited as Sean and Rhiana reluctantly left the room. "How good a friend Chuck is would be none of your business, Dean. Now what did you need?"

He beckoned her out of the room and into the foyer.

"Sorry, Chuck. I'll be right back," she said as she followed Dean.

Carly's house was a nice size for three people, but it wasn't a huge mansion. Even though they'd rounded the corner into the foyer and he couldn't see them, Chuck could still hear every word.

"It's about my visitation," her ex said quietly. "I'm going out of town and won't be able to have the kids until the third week in February."

She did the calculations, and knew why he'd cleared an escape route. "You'll be out of town for four weeks?"

"Close enough. Then we have a few weekend obligations, so I thought it would just be easier if I waited until after they're all done. Otherwise, the kids sit alone at my place."

"Easier on you, maybe. But not easier on your kids, Dean."

Chuck noticed she didn't mention herself. She wasn't complaining that she wouldn't have any time off. She was simply fighting for what was best for her kids.

"Listen, Carly, I'm a busy man, and I can't—"

"Dean, I had to listen to this when we were married, but I don't any more. And I won't. I can't make you take the kids. I can't make you want to take them. Do what you have to, and you'll have to live with the consequences."

"If you badmouth me to them—"

There was a warning in the man's words, and Chuck wanted nothing more than to go out into the hall and stand by Carly's side. But he knew she wouldn't thank him for it, so he held his place.

Carly made it evident she didn't need his help. "How could you dare suggest I'd badmouth you? Even when we were married, I made your excuses. I tried to be sure Rhiana and Sean didn't feel as if you had better things to do than spend time with them. I tried to convince them that you cared. Even at Christmas—"

"You're never going to let me live that down, are you?"

Chuck could hear the mounting anger in Carly's ex's tone. He stood, poised to hurry in with help if she needed him.

"There's nothing to live down, Dean. You've made your own choices. I won't badmouth you to the kids. I never have, and I never will. But they're smart. Smart enough to realize how their father ranks when compared to their friends' fathers. You never come to school functions, rarely come to any of their activities or sports."

"Oh, here it comes, Saint Carly and her litany of my sins."

"I'm not going to do this, Dean. You'll do what you have to, and I'll pick up the pieces. I've had years of experience."

"Have you ever thought that maybe it's your holier-than-thou attitude that ended our marriage?" Dean's tone implied the question was intended to hurt Carly.

But Chuck didn't hear any pain as she laughed mirthlessly.

"No, Dean. I'm pretty sure finding your secretary naked on my couch is what ended our marriage."

"I'm going."

"Do you want to go up and tell the kids goodbye first?"

"I already told them goodbye."

"Call them, okay? They'll miss you."

"When I have time."

Chuck heard the front door open and slam shut.

He still wanted to go to Carly, but she'd insisted she needed to stand on her own two feet, so he waited for her to come to him.

CARLY STOOD THERE, after Dean closed the door, trying to get her anger under control before she turned and took the too-few steps back into the living room.

Chuck was standing where she'd left him.

"Hey, you okay?" he asked. "I wasn't trying to eavesdrop, there was just no way to avoid overhearing—"

"No problem. It's no secret that Dean's..." She remembered her promise not to badmouth him, and finished, "He's just Dean. I'm trying to learn to accept him as he is, and let go of the image I have of who he could be—the kind of father that Rhiana and Sean deserve."

She felt oddly empty. There was no more anger at Dean. No more anger at herself for not seeing him for who he was. There was only a sense of relief that she was over Dean Lewis.

Chuck came and gently ran a finger down the line of her jaw. "So, will the kids be okay?"

"I'll see to it that they are." That was a promise. Carly couldn't make Dean change, but she'd do what she could to protect her kids. She tried to love them enough to make up for their father's lack of interest.

"And you?" Chuck asked gently. "Will you be okay?"

"Yes, I will. I always am. I'm afraid, however that this may throw a wrench into the two of us repeating this weekend's activities anytime soon."

"Let's not worry about us now," Chuck said. "Why don't you go up and check on the kids, and then I'll take you all out to supper."

"You're sure?"

"Positive. When I make a promise, I keep it."

She kissed his cheek. "You're a rare man, Chuck Jefferson."

"Not really, but I don't mind you thinking so."

She laughed. "We'll be down in a few minutes."

Both of the kids were in Rhiana's room looking far too serious for seventh graders.

Carly tried to infuse a generous dose of jolliness in her voice as she said, "Hey, my friend asked if we'd like to go out for dinner."

Rhiana ignored all mention of the invitation and zeroed in on what they'd obviously been talking about. "What did Dad say?"

"He's not going to be taking you for a few weekends, but—"

"Don't, Mom." Normally mellow, Sean's voice was sharp. "Don't make any more excuses for him. We get it."

"Dad's got better things to do," Rhiana finished for her brother. "We've talked about it. We understand that's just how he is. And before you get that worried look on your face, we're okay."

"Kids, your father loves you in his own way." He did. Carly knew he did.

"In his own way," Rhiana said. "He's seen more of us these last few months than he did when you guys were married. We've figured it would ease off eventually."

"And that's fine, Mom," Sean assured her. "This way we'll get to hang out with our friends on the weekends."

"Dad didn't like to drive us anywhere, and his new place is on the west side. None of our friends lived close enough to give us a ride. And to be honest—" Rhiana's voice dropped, as if somehow Dean might overhear "—Dad's house was sort of boring."

"You know him. He works all week at work, then works some more on the weekends at home," Sean said. "He didn't like us watching TV because it made it hard to concentrate."

"So we did a lot of reading." Rhiana laughed. "And before you tell me reading's good for me, I know it is. But come on, Mom. I've been reading almost a book a day when we're at Dad's. That's not natural."

Both kids laughed, and after a moment's hesitation, so did Carly, even though she was kicking herself for not realizing that Dean was giving the kids grief about rides. She figured they were so busy with their father that they hadn't made a lot of other plans.

"You two should have said something. I'd have talked to your father for you."

"Mom," Sean said, "Rhi and I have it handled. You don't need to worry."

"You worry too much," Rhiana agreed.

"So what about this cop taking us to dinner?" Sean said in a blatant attempt to change the subject.

Carly was willing to oblige him, but first she grabbed both kids and hugged them. As they squirmed, Sean screamed, "Oh, gross." They were growing up fast. Five more years and they'd be off to college.

She wondered if Dean knew what he was missing, and doubted it.

"Okay, so you two unpack and we'll go eat," she said and headed downstairs to check on Chuck.

WHILE CARLY WAS UPSTAIRS with the kids, Chuck went back to browsing her dance preparations. He'd already checked off Security for her.

The list was pretty detailed. It even included decoration suggestions from last year's committee chair. Carly had scribbled down, "Find time to shop." Maybe she'd like some help for that, too?

Man, he'd just considered voluntarily shopping and that wasn't something Chuck was proud of.

"What's that grin for?" Carly asked as she came into the room.

"I was still looking at your Valentine's to-do list and saw where you'd scribbled, 'Find time to shop.' I thought about volunteering to help, then remembered I hate shopping."

"Chuck, I can shop for decorations on my own. I do appreciate the offer to provide security. That's one big job crossed off my list."

"But Carly, the thing is, as much as I hate to shop, I don't think I'd mind if I was doing it with you." He held up a hand. "I know how that sounded, so you don't have to tease."

"Teasing wasn't what I had in mind. Kissing you was." As if on cue they both heard the kids racing down the stairs. "And since we're about to be interrupted, I guess I was teasing by offering a kiss."

Carly gave her kids a look that Chuck recognized. His own mother had given it to him. It was a warm, mushy sort of look that spoke of pride and, more importantly, it spoke of love.

"We put everything away, Mom." Carly's daughter said.

"And by 'put away,' you mean you've hung up all the clean clothes, and put all the dirty ones in the hamper?"

"Nah," her son said. "We shoved our bags in our closets and closed the door."

When Carly shot him a look he laughed. "Hey, you say you like it when I'm honest."

She shook her head and tried to seem stern, but Chuck could see her amusement creeping around the edges of her expression. "Well, Lieutenant, are we ready for dinner?"

"You can call me Chuck," he said. "The only people who really call me Lieutenant Jefferson are the reporters. Everyone else just calls me Chuck."

Both kids looked to Carly for permission and she gave the slightest nod.

"Chuck," Sean said, trying his first name on for size. "So you're really a cop?"

"Yes. I have the badge and everything to prove it."

"And do you get to ride in a police car with all the lights and sirens going and chase people around the city? And when you catch them, do you say, 'Stop, I'm a cop' and then throw them against a car, pat them down and handcuff them?"

"Mainly these days, I'm in the office. I drive a police car, but it looks like a regular car. And even when I was on the street, I didn't throw people against anything." When the boy looked disappointed, he added, "But I did pat them down and handcuff them, and my car does have a radio, lights and sirens, too. It's just that if it looks like a regular car, no one knows I'm a cop until it's too late."

That seemed to help his image in Sean's eyes. "Wow. Do you think sometime…" Sean hesitated.

"Sometime?" Chuck prompted.

"Well, I'm not supposed to invite myself anywhere, 'cause

it's rude, but maybe if you came over, and drove your police car you'd let me sit in it and show me how things work?"

"Sure." He glanced at Carly who was frowning. "Hey, he didn't invite himself anywhere. He asked to sit in it if I was here, and that would probably involve *me* inviting myself over to your house, so I'd be rude, not Sean."

"That's convoluted logic," Carly said, but she laughed and Sean gave Chuck a grateful look.

"And yes, I suppose that would be fine as long as it's okay with your mother."

"Oh, Mom will let me. She believes in letting us check things out, right Rhi?"

The girl nodded.

"Hi, Rhiana. Nice to meet you, too." Both kids were almost as tall as Carly, and though Chuck would never mention it to her, they'd probably both surpass her height soon.

The thing was, he rarely noticed how tiny Carly truly was. Five three, tops.

Maybe he didn't notice because Carly seemed to live life with gusto. And when you lived life in such a big way, things like height weren't always apparent.

"Your mom and I were working on the safety stuff and I invited all of you out to dinner, if you don't mind eating with a cop."

"Mind?" Sean said. "You can tell me all sorts of gruesome stories about being on the street. I watch *Law and Order* and *CSI*, so I know it's bad."

"I hate to burst your bubble, but real-life police work isn't quite what it's like on television." Again the boy looked disappointed. And given the kid's day, Chuck wasn't about to let that stand. "Wait though, I bet I can think of a couple stories you might enjoy."

He turned to the quieter Rhiana. "You don't mind?"

"No. Maybe I want to be a cop, too."

"Girls can't be cops," Sean said with a brotherly scoff that Chuck recognized. He'd made that same sort of comment to Julia. And he was hit with a sudden feeling of loss over his sister. Sometimes the slightest thing would make him think of her and the ache would start. It made him feel for Anderson and made him wonder how his brother-in-law was ever going to recover from the pain.

"Girls can too be cops," Rhiana argued. "I mean, there's that girl cop on *Law and Order SVU*. She's tough. Right Chuck?"

He nodded. "Right. Some of our best officers are women."

"See, stupid," Rhiana said to her brother.

"Okay, that's enough of that," Carly intervened. "Sean, your sister can be anything she wants to be, just like you. Gender doesn't matter."

"I know something she can't be." Sean grinned.

Chuck didn't guess and ruin Sean's moment, but he knew what the boy was going to say. He remembered using the same argument with Julia.

"There's nothing I can't be," Rhiana said.

"You can't be a father." Sean doubled over, laughing at his retort.

"Who'd want to be?" Rhiana replied without a hint of laughter in her voice. "Our father sucks. I'd rather be like Mom, 'cause she doesn't suck at all, even if she makes me do my own laundry."

"Whoa," Carly said. "*Stupid* and *suck* are on the don't-say list. Talking badly about your Dad is there, too, just in case I haven't made that clear enough."

"But Mom," Rhiana said, a stubborn look on her face. "He does s— stink. He's not going to see us, and he's not going to miss us. You miss us when we're gone. You call every day when we're gone for just a weekend."

"He won't even call us once," Sean added.

"We can't control your father's actions. We can't control anyone's actions but our own, and the three of us are going to be kind, not use nasty language—"

"And go out to dinner with me," Chuck filled in. "Come on."

He piled everyone into his car and drove to Valerio's. "It's one of Mom and Dad's favorite restaurants. Personally, I love their pasta," he said as they found a table in the dining room.

He'd taken women out in the past, but sitting at a table for four, with two kids, was different.

Sean and Rhiana carried the conversation, talking about almost everything but their father.

He learned about the school's science fair. Rhiana was experimenting with plants and music to see if there was any difference in the growth rates of plants exposed to music. Sean was testing the heat output he could achieve with different lighting sources and a magnifying glass. Different watt light bulbs, the sun, a full moon. "I started a fire once," he proclaimed proudly.

"Just smoldering, actually," Carly clarified.

Chuck leaned over to her and said, "I guess the firebug doesn't fall far from the accidental arsonist's tree."

As soon as the words left his mouth, he worried she'd take offense, but she'd laughed.

Somewhere around the time of his last meatball, Chuck admitted how much he was enjoying the meal. He liked Carly's kids. They were polite…well, to a point. Sean's belch was probably less than acceptable in polite society, but Chuck had earned a few points when he winked at the boy and murmured, "Impressive," while Carly and Rhiana both let out a well-timed, "Gross."

"Dessert?" Chuck asked, wanting to prolong the meal.

"Yes," the kids answered in unison.

Carly checked her watch. "It is Sunday—a school night, and I know that Rhiana and Sean have homework that I'd be willing to lay odds they haven't finished."

Chuck didn't need Carly to fill in that her ex probably hadn't even bothered to ask, let alone encourage the kids to do that homework.

"Only a little," Sean wheedled.

"Not much at all," Rhiana agreed.

"And I'm pretty sure they have a mean chocolate sundae on the menu." He suspected that Carly had been offering him a way out. He could see it in her eyes. At his response, she smiled, and for some reason, Chuck felt as if he'd won something, though he wasn't quite sure what.

"Well, what woman can resist a chocolate sundae?" she asked. "But when we get home, all homework will be done immediately, before family game night."

Both her kids promised. Chucked flagged down the waitress and ordered four.

He picked the conversation back up where they'd left it. "Family game night?"

"It's—"

"Chuck," someone called from the entryway into the dining room.

"Mom, Dad." He saw the gleam in his mother's eye—that certain matchmaking gleam he'd seen before—and he suppressed a groan. Not because that gleam wasn't groan-worthy, but because he was aware of Carly's kids sitting at the table, and knew groaning at his parents' appearance wouldn't be setting a very good example.

"Why, Chuck and Carly," his mother practically cooed.

"Fancy meeting you here. And these must be your children, Carly?"

"Sean and Rhiana, these are Chuck's parents. Mr. and Mrs. Jefferson."

"Hi," both of the kids chimed.

"It's so nice to meet you both," Linda Jefferson said, the gleam in her eye even more pronounced. "And now I see why you canceled our family Sunday dinner, Chuck. You know, it's not even the end of January yet. You're not starting this new family tradition off very well. Next Sunday, bring Carly and the children."

"Really, Mrs. Jefferson, that's not necessary," Carly said.

"Of course, it's not. But I'd really enjoy the company of two other women."

Chuck watched Rhiana preen as she realized she'd been included as one of the women his mother was talking about.

"Frankly," his mother continued as she elbowed his dad, "my husband, Chuck and Anderson are less than companionable. They basically inhale their food then hurry off to watch whatever sport is available. Any sport. Even if they don't like that particular sport."

"Hey, there's no such thing as a sport a real man doesn't like," his father said.

Chuck added, "And we all have very good table manners." He realized he should probably try to save Carly. She was shooting him those help-get-me-out-of-this looks, but he ignored them.

He knew he'd really like an excuse to see Carly next weekend. They only had the two safety-program dates this week and then she'd be done with her community service. He'd already guaranteed that he'd see her at the Valentine's dance, and with his mother's help, he'd have next weekend locked in as well.

"You should see Sean eat." Rhiana pointed at her brother. "He's just gross. He even talks with his mouth full, and that's *really* gross."

"That's a lot of grosses," his dad said.

"He deserves them. And probably more." Rhiana turned to her mother. "So can we go, Mom? It's not like Dad's going to be taking us."

Carly shot Chuck one last look, which he again ignored.

She must have given up because she smiled and said, "Sure, we'd love to. And we'll bring the dessert, Mrs. Jefferson."

"Call me Linda," she corrected. "And that's very sweet of you and would be lovely. None of the men in my life ever offer to help cook."

Chuck's dad laughed. "As if you'd let us in your kitchen. I think she tried to teach Chuck to cook—"

"I did," his mother said with a sniff. "And to this day I've never figured out how he could mess up boxed macaroni and cheese."

"Too much milk," Chuck admitted. "I read one and one-fourth, not one-fourth. It was soup."

"Well, here comes a waitress with sundaes. We'll let you finish your meal. See you next week." His parents retreated to a table on the other side of the small dining room.

A table that was directly in Chuck's line of sight. He couldn't help but notice his mother's animated excitement as she talked to his dad, probably about him and Carly.

The waitress passed out the sundaes.

Rhiana took a bite, then said, "Your mom's nice, Chuck. Your kids are lucky. I bet she's the kind of grandma who takes them to Waldemeer and the beach. I bet she even takes them to the mall and lets them buy whatever they want."

"Rhiana, Mrs. Jefferson's not a grandmother," Carly told her daughter softly.

Chuck could tell by her tone that Carly remembered that his sister had been trying to have a baby when she'd found out about the cancer. She gave him a look of sympathy. Not pity; a quiet understanding.

He mouthed the word, *thanks,* then turned to Rhiana. "Nope, no kids for me. No wife either."

"Well, your mom will be a good grandma. I can tell. Me and Sean don't have a grandma—"

"Your father's mother is very much alive and well, so you do."

"She lives all the way in Cleveland. We don't get to do stuff with her usually," Sean said. "Dad was supposed to take us to see her for her birthday, but he went out with his girlfriend instead. So, Mom called her and took us to meet her in Mentor for lunch."

"And Grandma doesn't even like Mom," Rhiana added. "She says it's Mom's fault that Mom and Dad got divorced. That's not fair, although Mom says it doesn't matter what other people think."

"Yeah. She says it takes two people to make a marriage work, and it takes two to make it fail. But we know it was Dad."

"Kids, we've had this talk. I won't allow you to blame your father. When you're older you'll understand…well, at least understand better. Relationships, for good or for bad, do take two people."

"We know." Sean sounded less than convinced.

Chuck was aware of how badly Carly had been hurt, but to hear her defend her ex and try to reassure her kids…well, his respect for her continued to grow the more he knew her. "That was nice that your mom took you to see your grandmother for her birthday."

"It was," Rhiana agreed. "Mom told us she was going to study and sit at another table, saying Grandma would probably want some time with us."

"But it was really that Grandma doesn't like her much since the divorce."

"Hey, hey, time out," Carly cried. "A— Your grandmother does like me, and I like her."

Sean snorted.

"B— I really do need to study for my boards. And C— There is no blame for the divorce. Sometimes these things happen."

Both kids snorted this time, and Chuck could see a disagreement brewing, so he stepped in. "I'm sure your grandmother would love spending more time with you, but Cleveland's a long drive, especially in the winter."

"Maybe. But people *have* to love their grandchildren. And loving's not the same as liking. For sure your mom will like her grandkids someday." There was a wistfulness in Rhiana's tone.

So Chuck didn't assure her his mother would absolutely like her grandchildren and spoil them rotten. He wanted to do something to take away some of the sting of a grandmother who made her dislike of their mother so readily apparent, and a father who was content not to see the kids for an extended period of time. "Hey, Carly. I know they have homework, but maybe before I take you all home we can stop at my house for a minute."

"For what?"

"My city car's a take-home, so it's sitting in my driveway. I thought the kids might like a tour of the inside."

Thank you, she mouthed, and aloud said, "Well, if they eat their sundaes quickly and swear they'll finish their homework immediately after we walk in the door—"

"Sure," they both said, and Sean started eating his sundae at a very unsavory rate.

"Oh, Mom, you should know better than telling Sean to hurry," Rhiana moaned.

Chuck watched them with amusement, and caught his mother watching him from across the dining room. She had a huge smile and that knowing-mom look that so frequently drove him crazy.

What on earth had he started?

Chapter Nine

Carly didn't mind freezing in Chuck's snowy driveway, because it was obvious that Sean and Rhiana were thrilled not only with their police-car tour, but with the attention Chuck was lavishing on them as he answered all their questions.

Questions that continued on the drive back to their house.

"...and when you arrest someone, do you ever fingerprint them yourself?" Sean continued.

"Yes, I've fingerprinted them."

"Maybe, sometime, you could teach me how? I mean, I can buy an inkpad with my own money," he added hastily, glancing at Carly. "And if you showed me, I could practice for when I'm older and a cop."

Carly wondered if Sean had been thinking about it for a while, or if Chuck had inspired the new interest.

"I can definitely show you how to fingerprint someone. You know, there's a summer camp that the State Police put on every year, if you're really interested. I'm not sure how old you have to be to go, but I could find out."

"Oh, man that would be cool. Wouldn't it, Mom?"

"Yes, Sean, that would be cool. Please don't get too excited until we have more facts."

"Sure, Mom. I won't get too excited." They pulled into her driveway and all piled out of the car.

Carly fished around in her purse for her keys. She knew that Sean might have agreed not to get too excited, but too excited had already come and gone. The last time Sean had been this enthused about a subject was last summer when he was considering a career in marine biology. Carly could still recite the differences between toothed whales and baleen whales. Before this new interest ended, she'd probably know more about police work than she'd ever imagined.

"Hey, Chuck, do you think maybe you could bring your handcuffs over next time you come?" Sean asked as she herded them into the house and flipped on the hall light.

Chuck laughed. "Maybe I could."

Having Chuck and Sean talk about the next time they got together made Carly feel nervous. "Okay, kids. Coats and boots off. Rumor has it that your weekend bags are stuffed in closets, so they still need to be unpacked. Any dirty clothes need to be taken to the laundry room. Then homework. If you get it done in time, game night. If not…" She purposely left the end of the sentence hanging. She'd discovered an unknown threat was so much better than a real and concrete one.

"Can you stay for the game, Chuck?" Sean asked as he took off his coat, threw it at a hook and missed.

"If you want me to," Chuck answered before Carly could jump in and make excuses why Chuck shouldn't, couldn't stay.

Sean was nodding. "Yeah. I got more questions. Lots more questions for you." Sean bolted up the stairs.

"You've done it, now, Chuck." Rhiana hung up her coat and traced her brother's steps.

As they walked into the living room, Carly tried to tamp

down her irritation that Chuck had answered without even looking to her for a response. "Sorry about that, Chuck. I can make your excuses if you'd like to make a run for it." She hoped her annoyance couldn't be heard in her tone.

"Carly, I can't think of anything better than hanging out with the three of you for a game night. Well, maybe a couple of things that might be better." He wiggled his eyebrows at her in a comic leer. "Things we did at the hotel that we can't do now. But things I'd like to repeat at our first possible opportunity."

And just like that, her annoyance evaporated.

What was it about Chuck that could set her teeth on edge one minute, and have her laughing out loud the next? "Well, it may be a long wait for that first possible opportunity, considering Dean's out of the picture for a while."

"We'll figure out something…if you want to."

"Oh, I want to," she assured him. And she didn't understand just how much, until now. "I've discovered I enjoy having a boy-toy at my beck and call."

"Speaking of beck…"

"Hey, Mom, I pulled a button off my uniform shirt. Can you put another one on?" Rhiana called, interrupting all talk of beck and boy-toys. She peeked her head into the living room.

Back to the real world. The world that revolved around kids and work. Around buttons and comic-book runs. Around absentee fathers and laundry. Studying for her boards and planning a Valentine's dance.

"Sure," she said. "Bring it down."

"Thanks." Rhiana ran back up the stairs.

"You and I together is going to be a challenge." Carly warned Chuck. "My life is busy to the point of bursting.

Trying to find time for the two of us to have a private minute is going to be more than challenging, actually."

"Lucky for you, I'm *up* to the task."

Carly caught the double entendre and groaned. "That was bad, Chuck. Really bad."

"That's not what you said at the hotel," he teased.

"Well, I don't know that you know what you're getting yourself into, but okay then." She kissed his cheek. "Let's hope you're as *up* to the challenge as you think you are."

"I would have thought that after last night you'd have realized I'm always up for whatever comes my way."

"Worse, Chuck. You just went from bad to worse. Almost as bad as whatever you were going to do with that stray 'beck' comment."

"Now, wait a minute. That was brilliant—"

Before he could explain how brilliant the comment was going to be, Sean tiptoed into the living room. "Hey, Mom, I'm out of fish food and they're going to starve if I don't get them some."

"They'll have to wait until tomorrow. I'll add fish food to my list. Next time a bit more notice would be good."

"And Mom," Rhiana said as she came into the room with her shirt, the button and a small stack of papers, "you need to sign most of these."

Carly took the pile of papers. "Seriously, Rhi, we've talked about this last-minute stuff."

"Tomorrow morning would be the last minute. This is just not early. It's timely, even."

Chuck nodded. "Can't argue with her logic."

"You're not helping, Lieutenant," Carly scolded.

"Oh, you better watch out, Chuck. My mom loves using proper names when she's annoyed. Whenever I hear *Rhiana Stephanie Lewis* I know I'm in for it. And if she screams—"

"I never scream."

"—*Sean Baxter Lewis,* he runs and hides."

"Hey, I don't hide," Sean protested.

"Nothing wrong with hiding," Chuck assured him. "I'd hide, too. Your mom might be tiny, but she's tough."

"And scary." Sean's expression said he was teasing her.

Carly played along. "Oh, yeah, I'm scary. And I've noticed two kids who are stalling and not doing their homework as they promised."

Both kids turned around and fled. She could hear their laughter echoing up the stairs.

"I like them, Carly. You've done a good job with them."

People saying nice things about her rarely got to her, but hearing someone praise her kids always did. "Thanks. I think they're great, although I know that I'm biased."

She waited for Chuck to pick up their banter again, but instead, he simply leaned down and kissed her cheek.

It was as platonic as kisses come, and yet for all its non-sexiness, it moved Carly. Maybe because of its mere sweetness.

"You might be biased, but I'm an expert and having just met them, I can't be biased at all. Your kids are great."

Two hours later, Chuck roared, "I'm the king of this land. I hold a monopoly on everything. I either own the property or you all have it mortgaged. So, I think it's time everyone admitted their defeat."

"Seriously…what is it your mom called you? Charles August Jefferson? Lieutenant Charles August Jefferson—"

"Ooh, here it comes." Sean, who'd been his ally throughout the game, ducked for cover. "You're in for it now, Chuck."

"Uh-huh," Rhiana assured him. "Once she's invoked your middle name, it's all over."

"Chuck's in trouble. Chuck's in trouble," they taunted.

"So, apologize for being a poor sport," Carly insisted. She'd caught on that Chuck's act was for the kids' benefit, and it was working. They were both grinning from ear to ear.

"Come on, Chuck, apologize. We're young and impressionable," Sean teased.

"Dearest hooligans, I apologize for pointing out that you're both losers." He made an *L* against his forehead with his thumb and finger. "But not as big a loser as your mom. She's got nothing left even to mortgage."

"That's it." Carly picked up the pillow she'd been sitting on, and thwapped him soundly. "Come on, kids. Get him."

Melee was almost too sedate a description, he realized later. But when the pillow fight had exhausted itself, and Carly had sent the kids up to get ready for bed, she turned to him and said, "Thank you."

"For what? For being a bad sport and setting a horrendous example for your kids?"

"For goofing around with them. For going out of your way to see to it they had a great night…something that would lessen the hurt of their father's disinterest." She leaned over and kissed his cheek. "Just thank you. This wasn't in our boy-toy agreement."

"Hey, neither was another dinner at my folks'. Let's not worry about what we should do and what we shouldn't do. There are no rules, Carly. Let's simply enjoy ourselves." He pulled her close. "And, in case you didn't notice, I seriously enjoyed myself tonight." He paused and added, "Last night, too. Let's say this entire weekend was a resounding success."

"I think so, too."

"And I've been thinking about how we're going to find some grown-up time. I don't have to be at the station before the program tomorrow. And it doesn't start until nine. If you took the kids to school tomorrow, then came over to my place, we could ride to the school together…"

"I don't see how that's going to—" She paused. "Oh, before we go to the program?"

He nodded. "I'll bet we can find thirty or forty minutes. I know that's not a lot, but it may be enough."

"I planned on driving to the school early and studying for my boards."

He could sense her indecision. "Studying or me? You choose."

Carly hesitated a moment too long.

She was going to say no. That she'd better study.

And as much as he was disappointed, he would understand. "Hey, don't worry. We'll find another time. Studying comes first. That's what my mother always told me. I'll just see you at the school and we'll figure something else out."

"I'll find some other time to study. I still have a few weeks before my boards." She kissed him. "I'll be at your place right after I drop the kids off tomorrow. I can't believe there are only two more presentations to give."

Chuck couldn't believe it either. It was great to have a built-in reason to see Carly. He knew she was busy, which meant that once her community service was over, spending time with her might get more difficult.

Of course, she'd already agreed to dinner at his folks on Sunday, and he was working security for the Valentine's Day dance.

Still…

"Earth calling Chuck."

"Sorry, I was drifting."

"Thinking about tomorrow morning? Because, I am. I'm

thinking…" She leaned over and whispered what she was thinking in his ear. And suddenly all Chuck could think about was having Carly to himself tomorrow morning.

WEDNESDAY WAS THE LAST presentation of the Safety Awareness Program. Carly sat in the gym of yet another school and let that idea sink in.

This was it—the last one.

She'd met Chuck before the Monday one, and now today's. But after this?

Carly had thought she'd feel relieved that one more thing was crossed off her to-do list. She'd paid her debt to society. Her record would be expunged.

But instead of relief, she felt…let down.

She'd enjoyed the program. Enjoyed working with the kids—talking to them and listening to them. She'd miss that.

Though more than the work or the kids, she'd miss having an excuse to spend time with Chuck.

Oh, she still had dinner at his parents this weekend, and he was providing security for the dance. But after that?

"…and then I rushed into the burning building," Bob, the fireman said.

Bob had been talking nonstop in between the classes that filed through the gym.

Carly had hoped to use the time to study for her nursing boards—to make up for the time she'd spent with Chuck in the mornings. She kept trying to steal glances at her flashcards, but Bob just kept talking and she forced herself to smile and nod at whatever he said.

She glanced at Chuck, across the gym and he looked up at her and smiled. It was a smile that spoke of things they'd done this morning. Things she'd very much like to do again.

"…the lady screamed, and I…"

Carly liked Bob. Although he was disturbing not only her studies, but also her very lurid fantasies about Chuck.

Both Monday morning, and this morning had been hasty, fun—and each time had left her wanting more. More time, more of Chuck.

"…and then I told him, it might work better—" He stopped abruptly. "Oh, here comes the next batch of kids. Our last batch."

Carly glanced at the clock. It was quarter after one. "Wow, the day went fast."

"I don't think it was my scintillating conversation that made it speed by."

She looked at him as he used the word *scintillating*.

He laughed. "I've got a good vocabulary, and *scintillating* is a great, highly underused word."

"I didn't mean to underestimate either you or your vocabulary. Sorry."

He laughed. "Don't be. Your mind was on other things—other people. Chuck's a lucky guy. Does he know?"

"Know what?" The kids had flocked to the first two tables, but a few were drifting toward Bob.

"That you're in love with him."

"I am not. Gee, first *scintillating* and now going all hearts and flowers. You're sure you're a fireman? A tough, rushes-into-burning-buildings-to-pull-someone-out sort of fireman?"

"You can try to deflect the question by getting mad, Carly, but I just call them like I see them…with my very impressive vocabulary."

She gave a very unladylike snort as three kids swarmed Bob's table and a few more came to hers. Yet Bob's comment stayed with her as she handed out her brochures covering everything from fire safety to head lice.

Love Chuck?

No.

Bob was confusing lust for something more.

When that last group of kids had left and Carly started gathering her things, Chuck came over. "So that's it. You're done."

"Yes."

"I'll sign off on the paperwork when I get back to the office and let Anderson know it's coming. He's going to push it through, so hopefully by the time you get your test results, you'll have a pristine record again."

"Thanks, Chuck." She nodded at the box of pamphlets. "So, what do you want me to do with these?"

"I'll take care of them." He grinned. "You have a while before your kids get out of school. I thought maybe we could get a coffee…or something."

She caught Bob looking in their direction and grinning.

Love Chuck?

She shook her head. "I'd love to, but really, I have to study. I work the next two days and—"

He interrupted. "Carly, that's fine. I get it. Maybe dinner?"

"It's sort of crazy the next few days. How about I see you Sunday at your mother's?"

He looked disappointed, and part of Carly wanted to say she'd changed her mind, but she glanced over at Bob again and didn't say anything.

"Sure," Chuck said finally. "I'll pick you guys up on Sunday."

"That's okay. I know where your parents' house is now. We'll meet you there."

Chuck's smile looked a little forced, but it was there as he nodded. "Great. See you Sunday, then."

Carly walked out of the gym, her debt to society paid and her independence from Chuck as clear as she could make it.

She should feel elated.

But she didn't.

She felt something else entirely.

Something she couldn't quite put her finger on.

"YOUR KIDS ARE ADORABLE and so well-behaved," Mrs. Jefferson said on Sunday.

The men and kids were all playing a very intense game of Wii bowling in the other room. "Having children in the house gives my guys an excuse to play."

Mrs. Jefferson was busy mixing a vegetable dip while Carly sliced the carrots and celery.

"Well, Sean and Rhi are enjoying the attention."

Mrs. Jefferson scraped the dip into the serving bowl. "I hope you don't think I'm being nosey, but I was wondering about their father? Is he still in the picture?"

Ah, there was a question. Dean hadn't called the kids all week, so how much in the picture did he consider himself?

"Yes, for the most part he is. At least, when it's convenient for him." She caught herself. "Sorry. I keep swearing that I'm over the bitterness. That I'm going to be that classy sort of ex-wife who puts aside her own pain, forgets the past and forges a new relationship with her ex for her kids' sake. I do try, but sometimes I lapse. It gets harder when he neglects the kids. Sometimes I want to shake him and ask him if he understands what he's missing."

Carly lopped the greens off a carrot with far more force than was really necessary.

Mrs. Jefferson stopped mixing the dip, then reached across the counter to pat Carly's hand. "Of course it's harder when you feel he's slighting the children. You're a mother and you just want what's best for them."

"Which is why I need to figure out how to get along with him. That's what's best."

"How long has it been since your divorce?"

Carly used to be able to answer that question down to the day. But as Mrs. Jefferson asked the question, Carly realized she didn't know. She was no longer counting. She didn't wake up each morning and think it's been so many months, so many days since her marriage had died. "A little over a year."

"Well, maybe it's fate. Kismet even." Mrs. Jefferson sounded way too flippant about the most traumatic even in Carly's life.

Carly's surprise at her tone must have showed because Chuck's mom said, "Oh, that didn't come out quite right. I didn't mean your divorce was a good thing, or fated, but rather if you hadn't married your ex, you wouldn't have divorced him and asked for the couch. And you'd have no earthly reason to burn it and start the fire…so you'd have never met Chuck." She smiled as if she'd worked out some sort of quantum theory. "I've never been one to believe in fate. We make our own fates. But your story has me near to believing."

"Mrs. Jefferson, I don't want any misunderstandings. Chuck and I—"

How to describe their relationship to Chuck's mother without crushing her newly discovered belief in fate. "Maybe I was fated to meet Chuck. He's become a good friend. He's done more to help me than you'll ever know. You raised a lovely man."

"Why, thank you, dear."

"But…" She paused until she was sure that *but* got Mrs.

Jefferson's attention. "But Chuck and I aren't destined for some fairytale romance. We're friends. Good friends. But…" she said again, then shrugged. "I don't want you to think it's more than it is."

"I've seen the two of you together. There's something there. Some spark."

Carly wasn't about to tell Chuck's mother that indeed there was a spark. Three days apart had definitely led to a combustible sexual tension from them and that spark threatened to ignite it at any second. "Ma'am, I don't want you to think there's more to us than there is. Any sparks you see are firmly founded in friendship. Neither of us is looking for a happily-ever-after."

"Fine dear, you don't have to look. But if it's okay, I'll be watching out for you."

"Mrs. Jefferson…" Chuck's mother smiled in such a way that Carly admitted it was hopeless to argue with her. She'd believe what she wanted to believe, until the relationship ended. "I just didn't want to lead you on."

"Don't you worry about me, dear. Now, tell me more about the children. Chuck said they're both in seventh grade?"

"Sean and Rhiana were born ten months apart, and Sean wasn't quite ready for school, so I held him back a year—"

They finished what they were doing in the kitchen and took the appetizers into the living room.

"Mom, we've gotta get a Wii," Sean said as Chuck's father swung his arm back then forward. The little avatar on the screen mimicked the move and a bowling ball spun down a cyber-lane.

"Strike," Mr. Jefferson yelled excitedly.

"See, Mom? We need one."

Carly wasn't a big fan of video games. She'd avoided

buying them for the kids, although she knew they used them at friends' houses. But watching Anderson take a turn proved that this one did look fun. "Maybe next Christmas."

"Next Christmas will be too late," Sean muttered. "Everyone else will have something new by then."

"We'll talk about it later."

Anderson's avatar got a spare. He beckoned her over to the couch. "I just wanted you to know, Chuck got me the paperwork right after you finished on Wednesday, and I've put it into the system. You should be a record-free citizen in short order."

"Thanks, Andy—"

He frowned. "I'd rather thought we'd gotten past the Andy stuff."

"I'll confess, I called you Andy at first to needle you. Now, I do it because that's who you are when you're here. In court you're Your Honor, or Judge Bradley. The rest of the world knows you as Anderson. But here, in the Jefferson house, among family, you're simply Andy. It fits who you are here."

He didn't say anything for a second, then he nodded. "Fine. When you put it like that, how can I complain?"

"Oh, you could complain, but it wouldn't do you any good," she teased.

"Are you two at it again?" Mrs. Jefferson asked. "I still have the time-out corners I used to use with Chuck and Julia."

As she mentioned her daughter's name, it was as if every adult in the room froze, waiting for Anderson's reaction. The kids, unaware of the tension, continued crowing about the game.

"Well, Carly started it," Anderson said, with the right degree of childish whine.

Carly might not have known the Jefferson family long, but she knew them well enough that the fact that Anderson was joking—that he'd heard his wife's name without freezing up—was something of a milestone.

Maybe that's what set the tone for the meal.

Or maybe it was Mrs. Jefferson's misguided newly discovered belief in kismet.

Or maybe it was simply having kids in the house.

Whatever it was, the Sunday dinner became a festive one. Carly and Anderson, and occasionally, Anderson and Chuck kept up a jovial banter, Mrs. Jefferson lectured all three of the adults on behaving and warned of time-outs, much to Rhiana and Sean's delight.

When the meal finished, they had another round of Wii bowling, before Carly proclaimed it time to go home.

The kids both moaned.

"Now, now," Mrs. Jefferson said. "It's not as if you won't come over again. We'll just have to convince Chuck to bring you all back soon."

Chuck's mom leaned over and hugged Carly. "I'm so glad you brought Sean and Rhiana. I hope we see you at more Sunday meals."

Carly didn't want to say yes, because she wasn't sure how much longer she'd be seeing Chuck. And coming to Sunday meals at his mother's felt too intimate. Too much for what they were. So she didn't acknowledge the blanket invitation. She simply said, "Thanks for inviting us. We had a lovely time."

"Don't be a stranger," Chuck's father said. He reached out and slapped Sean's shoulders. "You and your sister were good fun. You remind me a lot of Chuck when he was young."

"Oh, poor kid," Anderson teased. "Seriously, don't scare

the boy by telling him he reminds you of Chuck. That's just wrong."

"Nice, Andy. Better me, than you. I mean, Sean's already said he'd like to be a cop. How many kids his age say, oh, man, being a judge must be so cool?"

"I don't think anyone uses the word *cool* any more, Chuck. It's not hip," Anderson corrected.

"Come on, guys," Carly prompted, which put an end to Anderson and Chuck's banter.

She loaded the kids in her car. Then turned to Chuck. "Well, thanks again."

"Is something wrong?" Chuck asked. Carly had barely talked to him all night. She'd chatted with his mom and Anderson. Even his dad. But not him.

"Of course nothing's wrong."

"Then do you mind if I come over for a bit? I've got some stuff for the kids."

She nodded slowly. "Sure."

Chuck trailed Carly's van to her house, and grabbed a bag from the passenger seat before he followed them inside.

"I have a present for you," he said after they'd shed their coats and boots.

He handed the bag to Sean, then turned to Rhiana. "I know you weren't the one who asked, but I thought you might enjoy it as well."

Sean had already opened the bag. "Oh, cool." He thrust the bag at Rhiana.

She looked up at Chuck and smiled. "Will you show us how?"

"What is it?" Carly asked.

"I brought the stuff we need to fingerprint, and I have my duty handcuffs," he explained.

Sean crowed with delight.

"Just to show you," Chuck added.

"Yeah, I guess Mom would be mad at you if you let me keep them and I locked Rhiana up every time she tried to hog the bathroom. And Rhiana hogs it a lot, so she'd be handcuffed up a lot."

"Hey, I don't want you to think I forgot you." From his jacket pocket he took out a small plastic bag.

Carly took it gingerly and peeked inside. "Highlighters?"

"I thought it might make the studying go faster. It's a four-pack."

She gave him an odd look, then simply said, "Thanks."

For the next hour Chuck taught both kids the art of finger-printing while Carly flitted about the house, doing this and that. He knew how busy she was and wouldn't have minded her catching up on house stuff if he thought that's all there was to it. But it didn't take a detective to notice Carly seemed to be avoiding him. He wasn't sure why.

When they finished fingerprinting, Sean asked for math help and Chuck volunteered. He was pleased to discover he remembered enough algebra to assist the kids with some simple equations they had for homework.

Carly finally sat down at the table with them, filling out forms, making out the check for the kids' February lunches.

Chuck rather liked the feeling of the four of them all sitting around the dining-room table, working together.

There was a stack of nursing books on the sideboard. He caught Carly eyeing them as she got up to toss another load of laundry in.

"Hey, Chuck, are you leaving?" Sean asked.

"It's almost nine. So, I'd better be going soon. You two have school tomorrow, and I know your mom wants to study."

"We've got a while. We thought maybe you'd like another game of Monopoly? We can play the short version."

"There's a short version to Monopoly?"

"Well, we've sort of made up our rules in order to make the game go faster. The three of us can play while Mom studies."

"Does that work for you?" he asked Carly, who'd come back into the room with a basket full of clean clothes.

She looked uncertain. "Sure."

An hour later, game played, laundry put away, and kids in bed, he knew it was really time for him to go. "When can I see you again?"

"The next few weeks are going to be busy. My boards are just a couple of weeks away. I've got to study."

"Maybe I could help you study."

"I don't mean to look a gift-helper in the mouth, but Chuck, just what do you know about PICC lines?"

"Carly, let me help." He wasn't sure why she was trying to push him away. Normally, Chuck would take that as a sign that it was time for a relationship to end. All he knew was that wasn't what he'd prefer to happen.

"I'll bring dinner over tomorrow and if I'm in the way at any time, you can kick me out."

She shook her head and let out a huge sigh. "I was going to say no. I meant to say no. And yet, here I am saying yes. I'm not sure why."

Something had spooked her. Had his mother said something to her in the kitchen? Still, whatever it was, she'd said yes, and he wasn't about to pass up the chance to be with her, and the kids.

"Great. See you then."

And before she could say anything else, he kissed her

good-night. It wasn't nearly enough and a big part of him wanted to push for more, but he could tell Carly needed her space.

"Tomorrow," he said then sprinted out the door.

Maybe tomorrow he'd get to the bottom of what was wrong.

Chapter Ten

February

Carly had meant to tell Chuck no on Sunday night.

And she meant to tell him no again on Monday night, then Tuesday night…

It had been entire week of her *meaning* to tell him that no, she couldn't see him the next day. An entire week of saying yes instead.

She had managed to tell him she was capable of studying on her own when he offered to quiz her.

Which is why Chuck was at her house after dinner Thursday night, sitting next to her on the couch, going over some report for work while she studied.

Rhiana and Sean came running into the living room, and Rhiana asked, "Mom, after dinner, could me and Sean go to the basketball game at school? I bet we can get Mrs. Williams to give us a ride home if you don't want to come get us."

"Seton says he's going," Sean added.

"What time does the game start?" she asked, her plan of hibernating with her books evaporating before her eyes.

"Eight," Rhiana said. "We'd be home before nine-thirty.

And it's not like we're staying out late just to stay out late. We're going to support our school."

"Or I could just run you two down to the school, then pick you up when it's over," Chuck offered.

"Really? Thanks, Chuck," Sean said. "Can we, Mom?"

"That way, if Chuck takes us, you can study." There was more than a hint of wheedling in Rhiana's voice. "All my friends are going."

"Sure," Carly said. That's all the kids needed to hear. They both took off up the stairs. "You made their night. But really Chuck, I can take them."

"Why get all bundled up to drive them a few blocks? Put your nose back in your books. I've got it."

She hesitated, but finally nodded. "Thanks."

"Any time." He paused. "I can go home in between, or…"

She recognized that *or*. Or he could come back and they could enjoy having the quiet house all to themselves.

She looked at her books and knew that she should study for her boards.

Then she looked at Chuck.

"How long will it take you to get back from Erie Elementary?" she asked with a grin.

"A lot less time than you think."

He gave her a kiss that was a mere appetizer for what was to come, and abruptly pulled away as the kids came thundering down the stairs.

Carly looked at her books again.

Somehow she'd figure out how to get it all done.

She always did.

"…AND THAT'S BEEN MY two weeks since our last meeting," Carly wrapped up at the PTA social planning meeting the next night.

"Wow, you have been busy," Michelle said.

"And by *busy,* she means *buuusssy,*" Samantha teased.

Carly chuckled. "I know it sounds silly. I have two kids, so it's not as if I was in any way virginal, but that first night at the hotel felt so different because I took charge. I got the room. I made the moves. I feel as if I'm liberated, somehow."

Michelle passed her a tray of Romolo chocolates. Carly picked a small square and was delighted to find what was inside. "I love caramel." She sighed contentedly. "Do you ever have a moment in your life where everything seems to be going so perfectly that you can hardly stand it?"

"Caramel pushing you over the perfect edge?" Samantha took a chocolate. "Mint. I like mint."

"Caramel is just another indication of how well my life is going. My kids like Chuck. Chuck likes me and doesn't mind being my boy-toy. As a matter of fact, he's made it abundantly clear that boy-toyness is all he aspires to. And if everything goes according to plan, I'll have a date for the Valentine's dance—which is right on track, planning-wise—before we break up."

Carly ignored the memory of Bob saying she was in love with Chuck. Bob didn't know her. He had no way to assess how she felt.

Michelle and Samantha did know her, and both of them seemed convinced that the only thing Carly wanted from Chuck had nothing to do with love.

"Planning to break up doesn't sound very perfect to me," Michelle said.

Carly shook her head. "You're young and still in that initial glow of first love. Me? I'm older and jaded. A boy-toy with an upcoming expiration date is exactly what I need."

"That's what I thought with Harry. The fact he was an interim principal was perfect…until it wasn't." Samantha offered her a sage smile, as if she knew some secret that Carly didn't.

And if Samantha did know some secret, Carly didn't want to know it. "Well, Chuck's not leaving. He's just not the serious kind. And that's what I want. I want to be on my own. I don't want to fade into the shadow of another man's life."

"You want to find your own color," Michelle said.

Carly was surprised she remembered that off-the-cuff comment she'd made weeks and weeks ago. "Yes. I want to find my own color. I'm standing on my own two feet. So knowing Chuck and I are temporary is perfect."

"Although a second dinner with his family doesn't sound very temporary—" Samantha started.

Carly interrupted. "It's nothing. Besides, there was no way to say no—his mom's so nice."

"As long as you're happy." Michelle still look worried.

Samantha nodded, but didn't look overly convinced. "How goes the studying for the boards? Need some help?"

"I haven't studied as much as I'd hoped," Carly admitted.

She wanted to. But every night Chuck had shown up with dinner or for dinner. And then they'd both do whatever the kids needed. Homework, a game, or watching a show on television. Then the kids would go to bed, and she'd spend an hour or two with Chuck just talking. About their days. About their plans. About their pasts.

"I'm sure I'll find more time next week. I've pretty much finished all the Valentine plans. So, we're good there. Now onto the important business. How about the wedding plans, Samantha?" Carly asked, mainly to get them off her back about Chuck. She knew that one simple question would lead to a discussion that could easily last the rest of the meeting.

"Uh, I have a bit of an announcement," Michelle interrupted. "Daniel and I set our date. The second Saturday in July. I was hoping you'd both be my maids of honor."

Carly was happy for her friend, and joined Samantha in hugging Michelle. But seriously, how much romance was she expected to survive? Valentine's Day, Samantha's wedding. Now Michelle's?

And as Samantha and Michelle waxed poetic about their upcoming weddings, Carly tried to keep smiling. She didn't want her lack of enthusiasm for weddings, or her lack of belief in happily-ever-afters to rob her friends of some of their joy. They both deserved their days.

Even if Carly didn't believe they could last forever.

When Michelle had asked about her color, Carly thought about how many times she'd started to say no to Chuck, and ended up saying yes. Maybe it was happening again?

Was she losing herself?

The thought scared her.

CHUCK WAS BORED.

He'd cleaned and done his laundry, and even read an old report. He glanced at the clock.

It was only eight. There was no way Carly was back from her PTA meeting yet.

And because he didn't think he'd be able to sit still long enough to watch a television show or movie, he decided to start painting the foyer. He pulled everything off the wall, and spackled the holes.

Eight forty-five.

Carly might be home. He dialed, hoping that if she was home, she'd invite him over.

Maybe he'd invite himself. "Hello, Lewis house."

"Hi, Sean. It's Chuck. Is your mom home yet?"

"I knew it was you," Sean said with laughter in his voice. "She just came in."

Without covering the phone, Sean yelled, "Hey, Mom, it's Chuck."

"She said hang on a minute while she gets her coat and boots off. It's snowing hard."

"Yeah, I noticed."

"Me and Rhi were going sled-riding tomorrow. Wanna come?"

Before Chuck could answer, he heard the phone being jostled and Carly said, "Chuck."

There wasn't any hint of pleasure in her tone as she said his name. "Listen, maybe we should have a talk, but first, how was the PTA meeting?"

"It was fine. And I'm not sure what there is to say."

He was worried now. Carly's words were clipped. "I thought maybe we all could—"

"Chuck," Carly interrupted, "my boards are a week from tomorrow. I really have to study."

"Okay. No problem. Actually, tell you what. I know Dean still won't have the kids. So, why don't I come get them tomorrow afternoon. Sean mentioned sledding, or I could take them to see a hockey game or something. That will give you the house to yourself so you can spend some serious alone time with your books."

"I don't need you to take the kids. I'm perfectly capable of—"

"There's no doubt in my mind that you can handle it all, Carly. But I like your kids. I think they like me. Or I could take them to the station. You know Sean would go nuts. Rhiana probably wouldn't admit it, but she'd like it, too."

He heard her long sigh over the phone. "Sure. I guess."

"Is something wrong?"

She hesitated. "No. No. I'm just tired."

"Well, get some sleep. Have the kids ready around eleven."

"I will."

Before he hung up, he said, "No matter what you say, I know something's wrong. I'm here if you want to talk."

Maybe Dean was giving her more grief. Maybe…

He wasn't sure of the cause, but he hated knowing that Carly was upset about something. And that she wouldn't confide in him.

"Like I said, just tired. I'll see you around eleven tomorrow."

Chuck heard the dial tone before he could tell her good-night.

SATURDAY, WHILE CHUCK had the kids, Carly tried to study.

Tried was the operative word because concentrating on her notes and textbooks was hard when her mind kept circling back to what Samantha, Michelle, Mrs. Jefferson and even Bob, the fireman, had said.

All of them thought there was something more between her and Chuck than a temporary relationship. Something more than a fling.

And that's the last thing she wanted.

Carly had gone into her relationship with Chuck insisting it would be casual. Easy. No messy feelings or relationship stuff.

The idea that it was anything more frightened her.

So, when Chuck brought the kids home and asked about dinner, she made study excuses.

She waited for him to push.

To insist.

Instead he kissed her cheek and said, "Cram away. Call if you need me."

She didn't call.

He did on Sunday to see if they wanted to do anything, but she sent him to his mother's on his own.

By Thursday, he hadn't even called. Which should have made Carly feel better, but it didn't—she felt worse.

She took Friday off from the hospital and spent the day before her boards cramming, trying to be sure she had an answer to every possible question.

Her mind was filled with emergency triage policies, cardiac procedures and rapid sequence intubation. Potential questions circled round and round.

And yet one question kept coming back to the forefront of her mind, no matter how she tried to block it—what about Chuck?

"SHE PRACTICALLY DUMPED ME," Chuck told Anderson on the Saturday of Carly's boards. He'd called to wish her luck, but Rhiana'd said she'd already left. He had a sneaky suspicion she'd been there, waving her hands, indicating that Rhiana should fib. "There's no subtlety to it, either."

He and Anderson were at George's again for breakfast.

Anderson took a sip of his coffee. "When I think Carly Lewis, *subtle* isn't the word that comes to my mind. She's about as subtle as a brick through a window." He paused, then added, "Match to a couch better yet."

"Okay, so why doesn't she just tell me? Talk to me?" Chuck stabbed at his plate with far more force than separating a bite of scrambled eggs required.

"I think the better question, to my way of thinking is, why do you care?"

Anderson's question caught him by surprise. "Huh?"

Anderson leaned back in the booth and took another sip of coffee. "You've dated a lot of women since I met you, Chuck, and although you're generally the one to break things off, I know various women have dumped you first, so why do you care if Carly does the dumping? If it wasn't her, it would be you eventually. Given her recent past, it seems kinder to let her be the one to end things."

"But I'm not ready for things to end."

"Again, why?"

"I like her. I have fun with her."

Anderson raised an eyebrow and Chuck easily interpreted the look. "No. I mean, yes, sex was fun, but it was more than that. I genuinely enjoyed being with her no matter what we were doing. Hell, I even liked her kids, and I never imagined I'd be the kind of guy who would find hanging out with two seventh-graders a good time."

"You haven't really answered my question. You've skirted around the answer, but haven't quite hit it. Let's come at it from a different point of view. Remember Patty?"

"Yes."

"You liked her. The two of you had tons in common. But when she broke things off, you didn't flinch. When she started dating that other cop, it didn't bother you in the least. What if I were to say I was thinking about asking Carly out?"

Chuck didn't say a word; he obviously didn't have to because Anderson set down his coffee mug with a clunk and started laughing. "Chuck, answer the question. You've liked other women, had fun with them, and been totally okay with it when they ended it. So, why is Carly Lewis different?"

Chuck didn't spit out an answer this time. He pushed his eggs around on his plate, and thought about it. Why was Carly different? She made him laugh. She frustrated him.

In Carly he'd found someone he didn't have any urge to break up with—someone he didn't want to break up with him.

In Carly Lewis he'd found someone he could love.

Maybe he already did.

He wasn't sure when it had happened.

But the thought of losing her, of not seeing her, left him feeling more frozen than Erie in February.

"Other women have all become too possessive, too needy."

"That's not a problem with Carly," Anderson pointed out.

"And she didn't berate me when I had to work."

"A nice trait, too."

"I'm not sure where this is going with Carly. Though I think I know where it could lead. I'm not sure yet."

"It's awfully soon to be sure about anything other than you're not ready to lose her."

Chuck pushed his plate back. "I should probably go talk to her."

"Probably."

"I'll go now." He patted at his jeans pockets for his keys.

Anderson set down his coffee cup and stood, then dangled his keys in front of Chuck. "I drove, remember? I can take you home."

"No, just take me there."

For once Anderson didn't needle Chuck. Chuck was silent, too, as they drove the short distance to Carly's, other than giving the address. Anderson pulled up in front of her house. Chuck looked at his brother-in-law. "Thanks."

"Do you think she's done with her test?"

"It's ten now, and the test was at eight, so if she's not, she will be soon. The kids will let me wait inside."

"Okay. I'll hold on to see that someone lets you in, then go."

Chuck nodded as he got out and made his way to the front porch. He hadn't thought this through. Hadn't weighed what something as monumental as maybe falling in love meant to him.

Because what came next, what mattered was that he tell Carly that he wanted more time.

And what really mattered was that she was willing to give it to him.

He knocked and tried to feel confident about Carly's reaction to his revelation. Sean opened the door. "Is your mom home yet?"

"Mom," Sean bellowed and turned around, leaving the door open as if he expected Chuck to come in and shut it.

But Chuck didn't go in. He stood, waiting for Carly.

Carly must have been home for a while because she'd changed into sweats. "Chuck, what's up?"

What he meant to say was, *I don't want to break up yet. I think maybe what we have could be something lasting.*

Instead he blurted out, "I love you," without preamble or explanation. "I don't want this to be a fling."

She stood inside the house.

He stood outside.

Her expression didn't soften and get that warm, mushy look he'd seen her give the kids. Instead, she looked mad. No, not just mad. Pissed.

And he knew—knew what her response was going to be.

"No. That was not our deal. You're the one who told me that you don't do this kind of thing. You quit women who want—" she hesitated and then said "—that."

"Love, Carly. You can say it."

She shook her head. "I can't do this. I can't give you what you want."

"What have I ever asked you to give but yourself?"

"That's the problem. If you insisted, if you wheedled. If you put your needs first, I'd know how to deal. But you don't. You didn't. You ask. If I say no, you let it be. You brought me dinners because I was studying. You drove my kids to games so I could study. You folded a load of towels last week. You…you bought me highlighters."

"They were different neon colors…I thought with all the studying, you'd like them."

"I did," she said, though her expression didn't show anything remotely pleased. "It was thoughtful. Considerate." She looked angry all over again. "Damn you, Chuck. This was supposed to be a fling. You've gone and turned it into…"

"And that's bad?"

She grabbed the door and held it, leaving just a crack, as if he might try to break in.

"It's worse than bad," she told him sadly. "I need to concentrate on me. On figuring out who I am. I knew who I was when I was a girl. In college. Before Dean. Then my parents died and I got married. And it was so easy to be the woman Dean wanted. The woman who would raise his kids, decorate his house and office. The woman who would help with his career."

"I don't want anything like that from you."

"But don't you see? I want to know who I am now. I want to do what I need. What I want. What color I am on my own before I can ever think about anything more than a fling."

"And I'm not a fling?"

"Not if you say you love me." She shook her head. "Not by a longshot."

"I said I loved you. I didn't ask that you love me. I only wanted you to know." That was a lie. He'd wanted her to say she loved him, too. Wanted it more than anything he'd ever wanted.

With Carly there were no worries that the job might rattle the relationship, that what they had might fade. He knew in his gut what they had could last…if only she'd trust in him.

"You swore six weeks with any woman was enough."

"Carly, a lifetime with you wouldn't be enough."

"And that's why we need to say goodbye now." She leaned forward, without letting go of the door, and stood on tiptoe. Softly, so gently it almost broke his heart, she kissed his cheek. "Goodbye, Chuck."

She withdrew and shut the door behind her.

Chuck stood there stunned. What the hell had happened?

He turned and remembered Anderson's car was still sitting there.

He walked back to it. "Did you tell her you don't want to break things off?" Anderson asked.

"That and more. I blurted out *I love you.*" He paused and let the words roll out again. "I love you."

"So why are you back in the car with me?"

"Because falling in love is the last thing she wants to do. She fell in love and lost herself. Something about losing her color. Anyway, it's over." He sank back in the seat.

"Chuck." There was sympathy in Anderson's voice.

Chuck shook his head. He didn't want Anderson saying anything. "Just take me home."

Chapter Eleven

One week after taking her boards and breaking up with Chuck, Carly got to Erie Elementary early and started taping the stupid paper hearts to the fabric-draped, folded-in bleachers around the gym.

She yelled at the kids for using the word, and she'd really wanted to use something stronger, but settled for it. "Stupid paper hearts," she muttered. "Stupid Valentine's Day."

She hated the holiday.

Hated all thoughts of warm fuzzy love and happily-ever-afters.

She knew where ever-afters ended, with a blazing couch catching the neighborhood on fire.

"Stupid, stupid, stupid." That's what she'd been when she'd agreed to that first dinner at Chuck's house.

She went to the decoration box for more hearts—and kicked it. Kicked it hard.

"Stupid. Stupid. Stupid."

"Hey, hey, hey," Samantha hollered, as she arrived, Michelle right behind her. "We're here to help. Don't get violent with the decorations."

"We didn't forget. We're on time," Michelle added.

"I didn't think you forgot." Carly plopped on the floor by the now slightly worse-for-wear box. "I knew you'd both come."

"Then what is it?" Michelle asked, sitting next to Carly.

Samantha joined them both. "Did you get your results? If you didn't pass, it's not that bad. You can retake them in a month, I think. Hey, it happens. You've certainly had enough on your plate. No one would blame you—"

"No," Carly interrupted. "I mean, yes, I got the results, and I passed." She tried to muster some sort of enthusiasm. Had been trying to since she saw her score online on Thursday. "My first instinct, the first thing I thought when I saw I passed, was *I can't wait to tell Chuck.* Of course, I didn't."

"Why not?" Michelle asked.

She had thought about calling Michelle and Samantha all week and telling them about Chuck's declaration. But she hadn't. She'd simply…wallowed. That was the kindest definition what she'd done this week.

"I didn't call him because…"

Why hadn't she called? Many reasons. She hadn't told him because he'd said he loved her. Because he was no longer just a boy-toy. "I've barely started to rediscover me. I needed to end things before they became too serious."

She still didn't mention Chuck telling her that he loved her.

"Carly, maybe you should—"

"Don't. Please. I know you both want to help. That you want to comfort me. That secretly you're hoping I'll fall for Chuck and be as happy as you are. But that's not going to happen. So, let's not talk about this anymore."

She stood, reached in the stupid box and grabbed another handful of stupid hearts.

"Is he still doing security tonight?" Samantha asked.

"I called the station and spoke to some cop named Kirk who said he'd come instead."

"Well, then, that's that." Michelle got up and held a hand out to help Samantha up. "Let's decorate this gym."

Carly ignored the look the two of them shared. It was full of sympathy and concern. She asked, with as much teasing as she could muster, "So, who was it that thought assigning me Valentine's Day would be a good idea?"

She knew her laughter sounded forced, just as Samantha's and Michelle's did. There was no mirth in any of them.

But they played along.

"Let's blame Heidi," Samantha said. "She's the one who roped us into this committee, after all."

"She's also the reason I have you two in my life. I'm not blaming Heidi. I'm blaming myself. I knew better than to date Chuck. If it hadn't been for—" she paused "—Anderson. Judge Anderson Bradley. That's who I'm going to blame."

She kicked the box again. "Stupid Andy and his stupid community service."

Samantha kicked the box. "Stupid Andy."

Michelle kicked the box so lightly it could hardly be called a tap. "Stupid Andy." She knelt down and straightened it. "Okay, no more kicking the poor decorations."

"Can I kick Andy next time I see him?"

Michelle looked up and had a genuine smile on her face. "Sure."

"Great." If it wasn't for Judge Anderson Bradley, Carly would never have had to deal with Chuck falling in love with her.

And maybe, just maybe, a little voice whispered—as it had all week—falling a little in love with him in return.

So, what was she going to do about it?

AT SIX O'CLOCK THAT NIGHT, with the lights turned down and the decorations in place, it was hard to remember they were in a gym.

Carly ran around taking care of last-minute arrangements.

She glanced at the clock and smoothed imaginary wrinkles from her simple black slacks. She'd thrown on a red sweater, not because of any need to dress for the holiday, but because she knew reds and pinks were going to abound tonight, and by fitting in she'd blend in. And maybe if she blended enough, Michelle and Samantha wouldn't notice how utterly miserable she was.

The band and security would be here soon. The dance would start and a few hours later, they'd clean up and it would be done.

She'd be done with the Valentine's Dance.

The Social Planning Committee would be finished.

Carly's life was about to find a new sense of order. She was an RN. She was still working at the hospital, but had put in applications for a few other jobs.

The one she was most hopeful for was with the school district. Because of the Safety Awareness Program she'd discovered she liked working with the kids. And being a school nurse would put her on the same schedule as Sean and Rhiana.

She was sure she'd find something, but getting that job was what she was hoping for.

Her kids were her priority.

She'd proven so much to herself, and was rediscovering her own individual color.

So why wasn't she happier about it?

"Carly?"

She turned and there was Chuck, dressed in his dark-navy police uniform with all its brass and bars in place. He looked... good.

So very good.

She knew she'd missed him, but she didn't know how much until she saw him. And that annoyed her. "What are you doing here? I thought Kirk was going to take over for you?"

"I said I'd be here. I said I'd do it. I try to keep my word, Carly." He paused. "Is that a problem for you?"

"No, of course not."

He looked around the gym. "Everything looks great. It seems you and I are destined to spend a lot of time in school gyms."

"Yes, I guess we were." She almost smiled, but didn't allow herself to. "It seems appropriate that we end it here."

She could see her response bothered him, but he was quick to try and cover it up. He simply said, "Mom and Dad are coming. They're dragging Anderson along, much to his disgust."

She felt uncomfortable at the idea of seeing his parents and Anderson since she'd dumped Chuck, but she didn't say so. Instead, she nodded. "Okay, well, I've got to see if the band has arrived. Would you mind standing by the front door until things kick off?"

He looked disappointed. As if he'd wanted her to say something else. But he didn't complain, just said, "Whatever you need, Carly."

"CHUCK'S HERE?" SAMANTHA asked forty-five minutes later.

Carly repositioned a table, more out of a need for busy work than because there was anything wrong with the table's original position. "Yes."

"What happened to the other cop?"

She stopped fidgeting with the table. "It sounded as if Chuck told him not to bother. He said he'd promised to be here, and so here he is."

"Are you okay with that?"

She shrugged and tried to look at ease. "Sure. Why wouldn't I be?"

"Carly, it's me you're talking to. Although it could just as easily be Michelle. The two of us get it. We each went through our own rocky starts with a guy recently. But look how good that's turned out for us. Maybe you and Chuck—"

Carly shook her head. "I'm so glad it worked out for you and Michelle, but Chuck and I won't be getting a fairy-tale ending."

"If you say so."

She did. She said so and meant it. She wasn't ready to fall in love with anyone. She still had so much to do, to discover about herself and about making it on her own.

She started to walk away. She could go check on the food.

Samantha reached out and took her hand. "Carly."

Reluctantly, Carly turned back to her friend.

Samantha dropped her hand. "You told Michelle and me a while ago that you wanted to discover who you are on your own…I think you've done that. And you've proven you can make it on your own. You said you needed to find out what color you were. I think you've done that, too. You're not standing in anyone's shadow now. But you are standing in the shadow of your past. Maybe it's time to step back into the light. And maybe you'd find that whatever color you choose to be will shine a bit brighter with Chuck at your side."

Samantha frowned. "I know how that sounded, but I also know you know what I'm talking about." Her friend left her and walked away. Then stopped in her tracks, turned around and added, "I never thought I'd say this, but Carly, you're afraid. And you're going to let that fear rob you of something special."

And with that, Samantha did leave Carly standing alone in the center of a sea of hearts and cupids with no idea what she was going to do about it.

AN HOUR INTO THE dance, Chuck was asking why on earth the
school had wanted security. The adults attending the event
were a sedate group, visiting at tables, some dancing.

He wandered over to his parents' table, where Anderson
sat looking more miserable than Chuck felt.

"So, go talk to her," Chuck's mother badgered him.

Why on earth he'd ever agreed to let them come to the
dance, he wasn't sure. His mother had moved from lobbying
for him to find a woman—any woman—to lobbying for him
to win over Carly. And since subtlety wasn't his mother's
strongest suit—okay it wasn't her suit at all—she'd spent the
last week advising him on how to get Carly back.

Chuck glanced away. "She's made her position clear, Mom."

"You told me. She's worried about color and being hurt
again. I don't really understand it—"

"That makes two of us."

"—but I know when a woman's in love, and Carly Lewis
is in love with you. And Chuck, I'm your mom. I recognize
those same signs in you. You love her."

"She was hurt and doesn't want to tie herself to any man
again. I don't know that she can trust—"

"Chuck, you're too smart to believe that. Carly does trust
you. As a mother, I guarantee that if she didn't, she'd have
never allowed you to go near her kids. Come on, Charles
August Jefferson. Reason this out. She trusts you, but…"

"She doesn't trust herself, her own judgment," he
murmured. And suddenly he understood. She'd trusted her
husband. Done everything he asked her to—to the point of
losing herself—and he'd still betrayed her.

Carly might love him, but she'd never admit it because
didn't trust her own judgment.

"And you," his mother said, obviously not finished yet.

"For years you've used being a cop as an excuse, but the fact you've never settled down has nothing to do with the occasional rocky relationship police officers face. That was never the reason. The problem was, you hadn't found the right woman…until now."

"Mom…" He didn't know what to say, other than to tell his mother she was right, and no good ever came from telling her that.

"Chuck," his father, normally silent about all things relationship oriented, said, "Your mother's right. You love Carly, and like it or not, she loves you."

"I'm a judge," Anderson piped in. "I read people for a living, and I'm with your parents on this one, Chuck. The question is, are you going to let her get away?" Anderson's voice dropped. "I know what it is to have lost someone you love, meanwhile you'll just throw away what you could have with Carly? I thought I knew you better than that."

"Go get her, son," his mother encouraged. "I think that may be your song."

As if it were a sign, the band started to play Jimmy Buffet's "Margaritaville."

CARLY STOOD ON the stage, peeking from behind a curtain, trying to judge the gym with unjaundiced eyes. The decorations looked lovely. Especially the Mylar hearts she'd used as centerpieces on each table. The metallic silver and red sides flashed in the candlelight as dancers wove to and fro dancing to "Margaritaville."

Daniel and Michelle.

Harry and Samantha.

Mr. and Mrs. Jefferson were even out there.

"Damn," she muttered. The song made her think of Chuck.

Everything made her think of Chuck.

She missed him.

She wanted to run to him and tell him so, wanted so much to take a chance on him. On them. It had been easier to ignore the urges when she didn't have to see him. But now…with him somewhere in the gym, it was harder.

She scanned the crowd, looking for him. She spotted Anderson, sitting in a quiet corner by himself, watching the dancers. She wondered if he was thinking about his wife, missing her.

Like she was missing Chuck. It was a tangible ache. She wanted nothing more than to find him and—

"Here you are."

She turned around. As if he'd known she was thinking about her, there he was. "Did you need something, Chuck?" Even to her own ears she sounded far too stiff and formal.

"Yes."

Rather than tell her what it was he needed, he closed the distance between them, and reached for her.

Carly took a step back. "Chuck, we've been over this."

"No, you've been over this. You've given me every excuse in the book. Some convoluted talk of colors, standing on your own and not believing in love. But that's all a lie, Carly. It's not that you don't believe in love. I've seen you look at your friends when they're with their fiancés."

She turned from him, and between the curtains she studied her friends dancing. "Samantha and Harry, Michelle and Daniel—they're different."

"You believe that they're in love, that their love is strong enough to last?" She turned around and faced Chuck, then reluctantly, she agreed.

She did believe that Harry and Samantha, and Daniel and Michelle were going to make it.

"Then you believe in love." Chuck sounded as if that statement settled some argument she didn't know they were having.

"Okay, maybe for other people, but not for me. I don't think I'll ever be able to trust another man enough to fall in love again. Not even you."

"No. It's not me you don't trust. It's not even men in general. I thought it was, but now I know it's not." He paused and added, "Well, Mom made me realize that wasn't it, but whatever you do, don't tell her. Anyway, it's not me, and it's not love that you can't trust and believe in."

"Okay, Freud, why don't you tell me what it is?"

"It's yourself. You can't trust in yourself. You trusted Dean. You believed him."

She nodded. "And then he had an affair."

"No, even before that he lied to you in a thousand different ways. He asked you to quit college and help him through law school and promised when he was done it would be your turn. But it wasn't. He needed you to run the house, take care of the kids, make sure his life went smoothly. In your relationship, it was always about what Dean wanted, what he needed. You trusted that he cared about your needs as well, but he never did."

It was easier to look at the happy school couples than at Chuck, so she did. "I don't need you to psychoanalyze my life," she told him over her shoulder.

He touched her and physically turned her around. "Yes, you do. You do need me. More than you know. You say you can't love me, that you can't believe in me, but Carly, it's not something I've done, or will do. It's you. It's you that you don't believe in, that you can't trust. You've shown in the past your judgment is suspect."

"So, there you have it. It's a cliché, but I'll give it to you. It's not you, it's me, Chuck. See, I told you. Does that make our breaking up easier on you?"

He shook his head. "No. Nothing could do that. Carly, you can trust yourself and believe in me. I don't need someone to make my life run smoothly. I don't need someone to hang on my every word, to redecorate my office and yes-dear me to death. You've changed since you were with Dean. In my wildest imagination, I can't picture you yes-dearing me."

She snorted. "Okay, so you're right about that."

Chuck released her and she backed up.

"And I don't want you to. Carly, I just want you. I want you when you're sweet, and when you're not so much. I want you to have your job, crazy hours and all, and I'll have mine, crazy hours and all. We're both independent, capable people who've proven we can make it on our own. That means if we're together, it's because we choose to be together. Because we're meant for each other."

"Because we have what Samantha and Harry found? What Michelle and Daniel found?"

The question wasn't really for Chuck, it was for her. She wanted to answer no. It would be easier if she and Chuck hadn't. But she suspected they had. She'd been suspecting it ever since she broke up with Chuck.

"You don't have to believe in me, or even in yourself, though you should." Chuck took a step toward her, and this time Carly didn't back up.

"But you do need to believe in us," he continued. "In what we have. In what we could be."

"What about your six-week rule?" she asked.

"It was never a rule, it was how things were. My mother pointed out that none of my other relationships lasted more than six weeks because none of those women was the right woman for me."

"Chuck, I was clear about what I wanted…no, what I need and don't need. I have to stand on my own two feet. I won't lean on anyone else."

"Carly, I can't imagine you *not* standing on your own two feet. You're the toughest, most amazing woman. And a good relationship involves two people who are competent and able to stand on their own, but know they can lean on each other if they need to. I'm here whenever you want to lean, but I'm not looking for a clinging vine. I need someone who's not going to berate me if I have to miss a holiday because of work. Someone who knows I'd rather be with them, but that sometimes work has to be the priority. Even now that I work predominantly day shift, it's not a nine-to-five job, and never will be."

She didn't say anything because she didn't know what to say.

Chuck filled the silence. "I want you. I love you. That's not going to change, Carly. Let me know when you make up your mind."

She braced herself, waiting for him to turn around and leave, but instead, he walked over the ground between them, took her into his arms and kissed her.

Just as she started to fall into the rhythm of kissing Chuck, he pulled back. "Come and find me when you're ready. Just don't take too long, okay?"

This time he did leave.

It would be up to her.

He was going to walk away and wait for her to come get him.

She was in charge. It was up to her.

The thought was as freeing as when she took charge of making love to Chuck that first time.

She was in charge.

He trusted her to figure it out.

And he was right…the question wasn't *did she trust him?* It was *could she trust herself?*

She spied through the curtains. Her friends were still dancing. Two couples who'd beaten the odds.

Chuck's mother and father were still on the dance floor, too, looking as if they were made for each other.

And Anderson was still sitting alone at a table, watching everyone else dance. Alone. Mourning the woman he'd loved and lost.

He'd probably give almost anything for another chance with Julia.

Carly closed her eyes for a split second. What would he say about her fear keeping her from going after the man she wanted?

And she did want Chuck.

Was her fear greater than her love?

Suddenly, everything crystalized and she hurried away from the stage into the dark hallway. She turned right and started down the stairs—and bumped into Chuck.

He glanced at his watch. "You know, that took longer than I'd hoped."

Then he smiled, and she knew it wasn't because of his teasing, it was because he knew what she was going to say. "You only left a couple of minutes ago," she stated matter-of-factly.

"Yeah, but a couple of minutes of not knowing if you're coming after me is the equivalent of a lifetime." He paused and asked, "You *were* coming after me, right?"

She nodded. "For the longest time I tried to be perfect. I tried to be whatever, whoever, my ex needed me to be. When that wasn't enough, and he left me, I was terrified. But over the last few months, I've done more than go through the motions, I've got my life back. I've got me back. And you're right, what I've found is I can handle things, and I can take care of my kids on my own. I'm starting a new career, so I can support myself, too. And I deserve more than being someone's six-week fling. I know I don't need to rely on anyone. But I do want you. I know you find my color analogy weird, but, Chuck, I just figured out, unlike with my ex, I've never stood in your shadow. You don't want me to. You don't rob me of my color, you make it brighter, sort of like those neon highlighters you gave me. You make it brighter."

She kissed him. Kissed the man she loved. The man she trusted.

And because she finally knew she could trust herself, she said, "I love you."

"You're right I don't get the color thing, but Carly, I get you. You get me. We were made for each other." He stared into her eyes deeply. "And I love you, too."

Carly wanted to run out and tell Samantha and Michelle that they were right. She wanted to go out and find Chuck's family and tell them, too. But more than that, she wanted to take this minute with the man she loved.

"I think I hear another Jimmy Buffet song starting." She held out her hands, silently asking him for a dance.

The man she loved—who loved her in return—took her in his arms and they danced and danced and danced.

And it was a very nice Valentine's after all.

Epilogue

Midsummer in Erie, Pennsylvania, tended to be hot and humid, but today was beautiful. There was a steady breeze blowing in from the lake, which made it feel cooler than the seventy-nine degrees showing in the thermometer.

Carly sat between Samantha and Michelle at the bridal table, Samantha in a light-blue sundress, and Michelle in her fancier white one.

Carly was wearing a pale buttercup-yellow dress. Her bouquet of summer flowers was sitting next to her.

Daniel's yard had tables and chairs scattered around it and a potluck supper laid out beneath a white canopy tent. Kids ran all over. The last time she'd seen Rhiana and Sean they'd been in one of the trees that bordered Daniel's property.

It was the perfect simple wedding.

Someone started tapping a glass with a spoon, and pretty soon, everyone—including Carly—followed suit.

As Daniel leaned over to kiss Michelle, Harry came up behind Samantha and the other set of newlyweds—barely a month since their June wedding—kissed as well.

Carly wasn't the type of woman who cried in public. And yet here she was, tearing up at Michelle's reception, just as she had at Samantha's a few weeks before.

"Here." Samantha handed her a tissue. "I came prepared."

Michelle and Daniel's kiss didn't show any signs of abating. Carly dabbed at her eyes, trying desperately not to mess up her makeup.

As Michelle and Daniel finally came up for air, Michelle turned to Carly. "Carly, I need to tell you something."

"Okay." For a woman who'd been so thoroughly kissed, Michelle suddenly looked far too serious. "What is it?"

"I need to tell you that I didn't pick out the flowers in the bouquets on my own."

Carly looked down at the arrangement in front of her dinner plate. There was every possible color in it. Bright yellow and white daisies. Purple irises. Orange daylilies. Tiny carnations dyed the same blue of Samantha's dress. Deep-red roses, and creamy roses that matched Carly's dress. Green ferns were sprinkled throughout.

It wasn't a traditional arrangement, but it was beautiful. Bright and cheery and exactly in keeping with the day's celebration.

Carly wasn't sure why Michelle felt she needed to stop her wedding festivities to tell her that she hadn't designed the bouquets. However, after living through Samantha's wedding day, Carly had formed the opinion that all brides lost their minds on their wedding days and should be humored at all costs. "Well, whoever picked them out did a lovely job."

"The arrangement has pretty much every color we could find in a flower," Michelle told her with far more seriousness than discussing bouquets required.

Confused, but willing to agree with anything Michelle

said, Carly nodded her agreement. "Yes, it appears you represented all the primary colors and then some."

"Think about it, Carly," Samantha said. "Every color."

"And they're all very nice," Carly replied, still confused about why her two friends were staring at her so intently.

Michelle shook her head, looking disappointed. She stood. "Everyone, I'd like to introduce you to my two bridesmaids. A maid of honor and a matron of honor, if you will. Carly and Samantha."

The audience, looking as confused as Carly felt, clapped.

"Stand up," Michelle instructed.

They both complied and Michelle continued, "The three of us met because we missed Erie Elementary's first PTA meeting last September and we were 'volunteered—'" she air-quoted the word "—for the Social Planning Committee. And though we knew each other from around school, it wasn't until those every-other-week meetings that we became true friends. The three of us stood together as Samantha learned to believe in herself…and once she did, she was able to allow herself to fall in love with Harry."

Samantha wiggled her ring finger, showcasing the beautiful engagement ring that sat next to a wedding band.

"We were there for her last month when she married him," Michelle continued. "And they were there for me when I learned to believe in love, that what Daniel and I had was more than a relationship of convenience, that it was something that was meant to be. And as you can see, they're both here with me today as Daniel and I sealed that love in marriage. And it seems only right, that today, we all three stand together again as…"

Chuck got up and walked over to Carly.

"The bouquets were my idea," he said. "I'm giving you all these colors, Carly, because I want you to know you can pick whatever color you want to be. I don't care. I just want you. Whether you're red, yellow or blue. I'm in love with you, Carly. And I think what you and I have both learned is that it's possible to stand on our own two feet…as long as we stand next to each other. Sometimes I'll lean on you and sometimes you'll lean on me. We both have demanding careers—you're even starting a new job in a few months."

Carly smiled at the mention of her working as a school nurse, but she was sure that's not why Chuck was making this showy presentation.

"But," he continued, "rather than feel as though our jobs take us away from our relationship, we've learned that it just makes our time together all the more treasured and sweet."

He took a deep breath. "What I'm saying is, marry me. Carly, I promise to love you for the rest of my life."

Carly felt frozen to the spot.

Things had been going so great with Chuck.

Even with all her friends' wedding arrangements, she hadn't thought of anything more permanent for herself and Chuck.

She didn't want to rock the boat.

Yet there he was, with a ring in his hand, giving her a bouquet of every color. And she knew her answer.

"Carly?" he asked, because he obviously didn't know what she was going to say.

She glanced at Rhiana and Sean. They were both nodding.

She looked at Michelle and Daniel, so wrapped up in their hours-old marriage, and Samantha and Harry, whose marriage was only a few weeks older.

Carly had learned so much this last year…even more these last few months with Chuck. She had as many facets as there were colors in Chuck's bouquet.

Carly the mother.

Carly the nurse.

Carly the friend.

Carly…Chuck's wife. Yes, that would fit in quite nicely.

"For a while now I've been looking for my color, and what I've come to realize is I'm not just one color, I'm many colors. And all of them are brighter and better with you in my life. So, yes. Yes, Chuck, I'll marry you."

Later that night, Chuck held Carly close as they danced in Daniel's yard, beneath the full July moon. "We'll have to stop at Mom and Dad's before we head home. She's going to be insane about this. Just thought I should prepare you."

The music stopped and from the band's speakers came a female voice. "Hi, I'm Heidi. Erie Elementary's PTA President. I know that Michelle and Daniel have invited a lot of our school parents here tonight. And even though it's still summer vay-kay, I want to point out, that it's never too early to volunteer. It seems last year's Social Planning Committee members have all become a bit too busy to reprise their roles, so we'll have vacancies on that committee to fill…."

* * * * *

Harlequin is 60 years old,
and Harlequin Blaze is celebrating!
After all, a lot can happen in 60 years,
or 60 minutes or 60 seconds!
Find out what's going down in Blaze's
heart-stopping new miniseries,
FROM 0 TO 60!
Getting from "Hello" to "How was it?"
can happen fast....

Here's a sneak peek of the first book,
A LONG, HARD RIDE
by Alison Kent
Available March 2009

"Is that for me?" Trey asked.

Cardin Worth cocked her head to the side and considered how much better the day already seemed. "Good morning to you, too."

When she didn't hold out the second cup of coffee for him to take, he came closer. She sipped from her heavy white mug, hiding her grin and her giddy rush of nerves behind it.

But when he stopped in front of her, she made the mistake of lowering her gaze from his face to the exposed strip of his chest. It was either give him his cup of coffee or bury her nose against him and breathe in. She remembered so clearly how he smelled. How he tasted.

She gave him his coffee.

After taking a quick gulp, he smiled and said, "Good morning, Cardin. I hope the floor wasn't too hard for you."

The hardness of the floor hadn't been the problem. She shook her head. "Are you kidding? I slept like a baby, swaddled in my sleeping bag."

"In my sleeping bag, you mean."

If he wanted to get technical, yeah. "Thanks for the loaner. It made sleeping on the floor almost bearable." As had the warmth of his spooned body, she thought, then quickly changed the subject. "I saw you have a loaf of bread and some eggs. Would you like me to cook breakfast?"

He lowered his coffee mug slowly, his gaze as warm as the sun on her shoulders, as the ceramic heating her hands. "I didn't bring you out here to wait on me."

"You didn't bring me out here at all. I volunteered to come."

"To help me get ready for the race. Not to serve me."

"It's just breakfast, Trey. And coffee." Even if last night it had been more. Even if the way he was looking at her made her want to climb back into that sleeping bag. "I work much better when my stomach's not growling. I thought it might be the same for you."

"It is, but I'll cook. You made the coffee."

"That's because I can't work at all without caffeine."

"If I'd known that, I would've put on a pot as soon I got up."

"What time *did* you get up?" Judging by the sun's position, she swore it couldn't be any later than seven now. And, yeah, they'd agreed to start working at six.

"Maybe four?" he guessed, giving her a lazy smile.

"But it was almost two…" She let the sentence dangle, finishing the thought privately. She was quite sure he knew exactly what time they'd finally fallen asleep after he'd made love to her.

The question facing her now was where did this relationship—if you could even call it *that*—go from here?

* * * * *

Cardin and Trey are about to find out that
great sex is only the beginning....
Don't miss the fireworks!
Get ready for
A LONG, HARD RIDE
by Alison Kent
Available March 2009,
wherever Blaze books are sold.

CELEBRATE
60 YEARS
OF PURE READING PLEASURE
WITH HARLEQUIN®!

We'll be spotlighting a different series
every month throughout 2009
to celebrate our 60th anniversary.

Look for Harlequin® Blaze™ in March!

0-60

*After all, a lot can happen in 60 years,
or 60 minutes...or 60 seconds!*

Find out what's going down in Blaze's
heart-stopping new miniseries *0-60!*
Getting from "Hello" to "How was it?"
can happen fast....

Look for the brand-new 0-60 miniseries in March 2009!

You're invited to join our Tell Harlequin Reader Panel!

By joining our new reader panel you will:

- Receive Harlequin® books—they are FREE and yours to keep with no obligation to purchase anything!
- Participate in fun online surveys
- Exchange opinions and ideas with women just like you
- Have a say in our new book ideas and help us publish the best in women's fiction

In addition, you will have a chance to win great prizes and receive special gifts! See Web site for details. Some conditions apply. Space is limited.

To join, visit us at

www.TellHarlequin.com.

REQUEST YOUR FREE BOOKS!

2 FREE NOVELS PLUS 2
FREE GIFTS!

Love, Home & Happiness!

YES! Please send me 2 FREE Harlequin® American Romance® novels and my 2 FREE gifts (gifts are worth about $10). After receiving them, if I don't wish to receive any more books, I can return the shipping statement marked "cancel." If I don't cancel, I will receive 4 brand-new novels every month and be billed just $4.24 per book in the U.S. or $4.99 per book in Canada. That's a savings of close to 15% off the cover price! It's quite a bargain! Shipping and handling is just 25¢ per book, along with any applicable taxes.* I understand that accepting the 2 free books and gifts places me under no obligation to buy anything. I can always return a shipment and cancel at any time. Even if I never buy another book from Harlequin, the two free books and gifts are mine to keep forever.

154 HDN EEZK   354 HDN EEZV

Name	(PLEASE PRINT)	
Address		Apt. #
City	State/Prov.	Zip/Postal Code

Signature (if under 18, a parent or guardian must sign)

Mail to the **Harlequin Reader Service:**
IN U.S.A.: P.O. Box 1867, Buffalo, NY 14240-1867
IN CANADA: P.O. Box 609, Fort Erie, Ontario L2A 5X3

Not valid to current subscribers of Harlequin® American Romance® books.

Want to try two free books from another line?
Call 1-800-873-8635 or visit www.morefreebooks.com.

* Terms and prices subject to change without notice. N.Y. residents add applicable sales tax. Canadian residents will be charged applicable provincial taxes and GST. Offer not valid in Quebec. This offer is limited to one order per household. All orders subject to approval. Credit or debit balances in a customer's account(s) may be offset by any other outstanding balance owed by or to the customer. Please allow 4 to 6 weeks for delivery. Offer available while quantities last.

Your Privacy: Harlequin is committed to protecting your privacy. Our Privacy Policy is available online at www.eHarlequin.com or upon request from the Reader Service. From time to time we make our lists of customers available to reputable third parties who may have a product or service of interest to you. If you would prefer we not share your name and address, please check here. ☐

HAR08R2

HARLEQUIN® *Romance*®

This February the Harlequin® Romance series
will feature six Diamond Brides stories featuring
diamond proposals and gorgeous grooms.

Share your dream wedding proposal and you could WIN!

The most romantic entry will win a diamond
necklace and will inspire a proposal in one of
our upcoming Diamond Grooms books in 2010.

In 100 words or less, tell us the most romantic
way that you dream of being proposed to.

For more information, and to enter
the Diamond Brides Proposal contest, please visit
www.DiamondBridesProposal.com

Or mail your entry to us at:

IN THE U.S.: 3010 Walden Ave., P.O. Box 9069, Buffalo, NY 14269-9069
IN CANADA: 225 Duncan Mill Road, Don Mills, ON M3B 3K9

No purchase necessary. Contest opens at 12:01 p.m. (ET) on January 15, 2009 and closes at 11:59 p.m. (ET) on March 13, 2009. One (1) prize will be awarded consisting of a diamond necklace and an author's fictional adaptation of the contest winner's dream proposal scenario published in an upcoming Harlequin® Romance novel in February 2010. Approximate retail value of the prize is three thousand dollars ($3000.00 USD). Limit one (1) entry per person per household. Contest open to legal residents of the U.S. (excluding Colorado) and Canada (excluding Quebec) who have reached the age of majority at time of entry. Void where prohibited by law. Official Rules available online at www.DiamondBridesProposal.com. Sponsor: Harlequin Enterprises Limited.

V Silhouette®

SPECIAL EDITION

Kate's Boys

TRAVIS'S APPEAL

by *USA TODAY* bestselling author
MARIE FERRARELLA

Shana O'Reilly couldn't deny it—family lawyer
Travis Marlowe had some kind of appeal. But
as Travis handled her father's tricky estate
planning, he discovered things weren't what
they seemed in the O'Reilly clan. Would
an explosive secret leave Travis and Shana's
budding relationship in tatters?

Available March 2009
wherever books are sold.

Silhouette® Desire

BRENDA JACKSON

TALL, DARK... WESTMORELAND!

Olivia Jeffries got a taste of the wild and reckless when she met a handsome stranger at a masquerade ball. In the morning she discovered her new lover was Reginald Westmoreland, her father's most-hated rival. Now Reggie will stop at nothing to get Olivia back in his bed.

**Available March 2009
wherever books are sold.**

Always Powerful, Passionate and Provocative.

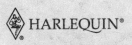

HARLEQUIN®

COMING NEXT MONTH
Available March 10, 2009

#1249 THE SHERIFF OF HORSESHOE, TEXAS by Linda Warren
Men Made in America
Quiet, friendly Horseshoe is the perfect place for Wyatt Carson to raise his young daughter. Until Peyton Ross zooms through his Texas hometown, disrupting his peaceful Sunday and turning his world upside down. The irrepressible blonde is tempting the widowed lawman to let loose and start living again. But there's more to this fun-loving party girl than meets the eye....

#1250 THE TRIPLETS' RODEO MAN by Tina Leonard
The Morgan Men
Cricket Jasper knows Jack Morgan's all wrong for her. But that doesn't stop the virtuous deacon from falling for the sexy rodeo rider. The firstborn Morgan son came home to make things right with his estranged father. Now *he's* about to become a father. Whoever dreamed it would take a loving woman with three babies on the way to catch this roving cowboy?

#1251 TWINS FOR THE TEACHER by Michele Dunaway
Times Two
Ever since Hank Friesen enrolled his son and daughter in Nolter Elementary, Jolie Tomlinson has been finding it hard to resist the ten-year-old twins...*and* their sexy dad. The fourth-grade teacher is happy to help out the workaholic widower—but getting involved with the father of her students is definitely against the rules. Besides, Jolie doesn't know if she's ready to be a mother—not until she tells Hank about her past....

#1252 OOH, BABY! by Ann Roth
Running a business and being a temporary mother to her sister's seven-month-old are *two* full-time jobs. The last thing Lily Gleason needs is to be audited! Then she meets her new accountant. Carter Boyle is handsome, single and trustworthy...and already smitten with Lily's infant niece. But the CPA has a precious secret—one that could make or break Lily's trust in him.

www.eHarlequin.com

HARCNMBPA0209